PUFFIN BOOKS

GOOL

Maurice Gee is one of New Zealand's best-known writers for adults and children. He has won a number of literary awards, including the Wattie Award, the Deutz Medal for Fiction, the New Zealand Fiction Award, the New Zealand Children's Book of the Year Award and the Prime Minister's Award for Literary Achievement.

Maurice Gee's children's novels include *Salt, The Limping Man, The Fat Man, The Fire-Raiser, Under the Mountain* and *The O Trilogy*. Maurice lives in Nelson with his wife Margareta, and has two daughters and a son.

PUFFIN BOOKS

Published by the Penguin Group

Penguin Group (NZ), 67 Apollo Drive, Rosedale,
North Shore 0632, New Zealand (a division of Pearson New Zealand Ltd)
Penguin Group (USA) Inc., 375 Hudson Street,
New York, New York 10014, USA
Penguin Group (Canada), 90 Eglinton Avenue East, Suite 700, Toronto,
Ontario, M4P 2Y3, Canada (a division of Pearson Penguin Canada Inc.)
Penguin Books Ltd, 80 Strand, London, WC2R 0RL, England
Penguin Ireland, 25 St Stephen's Green,
Dublin 2, Ireland (a division of Penguin Books Ltd)
Penguin Group (Australia), 250 Camberwell Road, Camberwell,
Victoria 3124, Australia (a division of Pearson Australia Group Pty Ltd)
Penguin Books India Pvt Ltd, 11, Community Centre,
Panchsheel Park, New Delhi – 110 017, India
Penguin Books (South Africa) (Pty) Ltd, 24 Sturdee Avenue,
Rosebank, Johannesburg 2196, South Africa

Penguin Books Ltd, Registered Offices: 80 Strand, London, WC2R 0RL, England

First published by Puffin Books, 2008. This edition 2010

Designed by Mary Egan
Typeset by Pindar NZ, Auckland, New Zealand
Map by Nick Keenleyside
Cover and map figures by Athena Sommerfeld
Printed in Australia by Griffin Press

ISBN 978 0 14 330544 6

A catalogue record for this book is available
from the National Library of New Zealand.

www.penguin.co.nz

MIX
Paper from
responsible sources
FSC® C009448

GOOL

MAURICE GEE

PUFFIN BOOKS

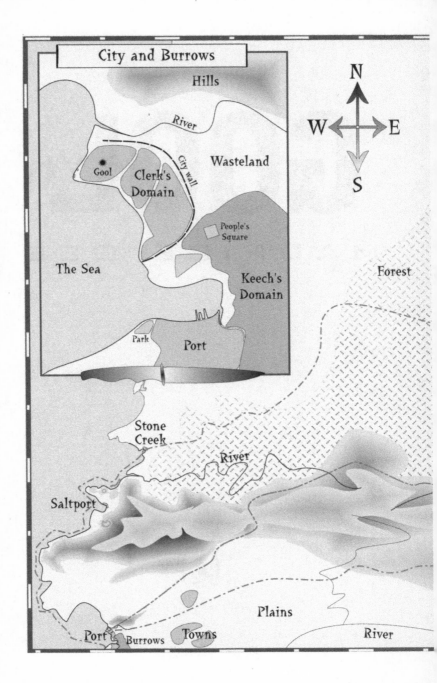

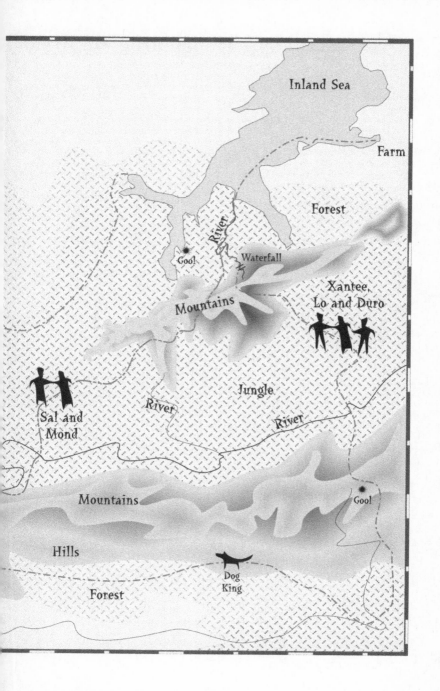

ONE

Hari had not been in this cove before but his knowledge of the Inland Sea led him to expect no dangers, either from the weather or from the close-packed trees in the valleys winding back from the coast. There were no thunderheads on the horizon, no edge to the wind, and no sense of darkness in the hills beyond the scrub fringing the beach. Three things Hari feared: sudden storms, unknown beasts, and dark places in the jungle where even the people with no name rarely ventured. But the schooner sat easy on a calm sea, the sand was yellow, the hills were blue, and the air carried a scent of blossoms.

Karl, he said, take Lo. Scout east to the end of the beach and through the scrub, then come back here. Keep in touch. Sal, take Mond; the same to the west. No need to climb the headland. Duro, take Xantee. Go straight in, not too far. I want to know if the trees start twisting. Stop if they do. Not a step further. All right, go.

They paddled away in canoes, six half-naked girls and boys – all but one as old as he and Pearl had been when they met and all of them 'speakers', rivalling the Dwellers in the ease and clarity of their silent talking with each other. Even Tealeaf, when she visited, found it hard to keep up with them, especially with Xantee and Lo. No one rivalled those two in quickness and penetration. The words passing between them went like the wind, like sunlight, opening spaces not even he and Pearl had the quickness to enter, although Lo and Xantee were their children, born from their love.

Who are they? Hari wondered, and what do they have to learn and what do they do? Questions that made him afraid. Beyond the Inland Sea, beyond the jungle and mountains, the world was in turmoil. He thought of it as a hissing cauldron, with a thousand unknown things, alive and tormented, throwing the steam and stench of hatred high into the air. This was all he could make of the accounts Tealeaf and other Dwellers sent back to the farm – and he thought: How simple it was in Blood Burrow, we knew what we had to do to stay alive. Here, by contrast, nothing was certain, all was rumour – of a beast born in damp caves and growing out of darkness into the sunlight, and of jungle trees twisting their trunks as though to escape from something evil.

He watched the children paddle away, Karl and Lo east, Sal and Mond west, and Xantee and Duro straight ahead. That pair was first to land. He had given his daughter the hardest task – if there was danger in the jungle it would be where the trees were thickest and not at the ends of the beach – and given her the oldest of the six, Duro, as partner. He was not her equal as a speaker but her alertness was sufficient for two. Duro's knife skills rivalled Hari's. If it ever came to fighting, with whatever the jungle held, Duro was the one he wanted standing by his daughter.

He watched until they disappeared into the scrub and heard the speech between them like an insect buzzing in the corner of a room, but did not bother to decipher it. Karl and Lo landed and walked east; Sal and Mond, trotting to cover the longer distance, headed west. West had a danger-ous sound to Hari. Company had come out of the west, that Company that had massacred half his people and enslaved the rest, and although it was destroyed now, and had become a memory, he never trusted it not to rise again on the western horizon in a black fleet growing like a poisonous cloud. Rem-nants of it remained, in the robber bands that roamed the countryside around the ruined city where it had ruled. Keech remained too – Keech of Keech Burrow, blind in one eye, but making up for it with a mind that saw round corners. He had united the burrows and ruled like a king, sitting in his rags on a throne of nailed planks. And the Clerk, who had been a Company clerk, ruled in Ceebeedee, but unlike Ottmar – Ottmar torn to pieces by dogs – was clever enough not to call himself king. Clerk was a more powerful name.

Hari shivered, remembering those places and times – yet his childhood never made him regretful or afraid. When he thought of Blood Burrow – the runways in the fallen masonry, the pits, the broken walls, the stairs leading nowhere, the swamps that had been parks before Company came, the marauding dog packs and the killing of rats for food – and Keech Burrow alongside, and Bawdhouse and Keg beyond, the word 'home' floated up in his mind like a trout rising in

9

a stream. It made no sense. The farm on the eastern shore of the Inland Sea was home – the fields, the orchards and gardens, the house with its spacious rooms and, even more, his family. Pearl and Xantee and Lo and the twins, Blossom and Hubert, were home. Yet here was Blood Burrow, so deep in him he would never get it out. He was not afraid and not regretful. He understood he could not be himself without his early years. Yet he wanted never to go back to Blood Burrow.

He wanted to see Tarl though – Tarl who had fled with his dog pack from the battle on Mansion Hill, across the drylands to the forest and through the forest into the jungle, where it was said he ruled, the Dog King with his thousand dogs, and all other animals under his control. Tarl was the father who had carried him on his back, fed him, taught him to survive in Blood Burrow.

Hari had sent messages: Tarl, I'm alive. No message came back. It seemed to Hari that his father might be long dead, with only his legend surviving. Yet still he hoped.

Hari shook his mind free of the past. He listened to the talk between Xantee and Duro – its tone alert.

Duro: No spoor.

Xantee: No scat.

Duro: Birdsong, though. Birds are here.

Xantee: That's a glassbird.

Duro: I've never heard one.

Xantee: Listen.

Hari heard it too, through them, a tumble of round notes on the edge of discord. Yet he grew anxious. If they both listened to the bird, who was listening for danger?

Xantee: I am, Hari. Don't worry.

Hari blinked. He felt he had been tapped with a finger between the eyes. How did they do that, Xantee and Lo? How did they know, across a distance, that others were anxious about them?

What does the jungle look like? he said.

Ferns, creepers, trees. I can't smell any darkness, Xantee replied.

Don't go in too far.

He turned his attention to Karl and Lo – Karl who made him think of buffaloes taking ponderous steps, and Lo, here-and-gone Lo, whom no one could keep track of, he moved so fast. Like a fangcat, Hari thought, but a fangcat without savagery, a fangcat that would soon be purring in the sun. Lo had growing to do, lessons to learn. Hari had put Karl in charge of the pair, not only from seniority, but because the older boy's love of the sea had made a quiet place in his mind Lo had had no glimpse of yet. The two worked well together but soon Lo would lead and Karl follow. Lo would join Xantee at the point of the spear.

Hari shook himself. He did not like the thoughts of conflict that invaded his mind, appearing more frequently these days with the news from over the mountains and the rumours of a creeping darkness in the jungle. He did not want his children to be a spear. He had made a home for them on the farm and he wanted them growing there with the other children, learning the skills of the land as he and Pearl had done, and raising families in their turn.

He watched Karl and Lo enter the scrub.

Anything there? he asked.

Sign, Karl replied. Swamp deer, it looks like. There's mosquitoes.

So, a swamp deeper in. There'll be snakes.

And water choppers, Lo said.

Be careful.

He turned his attention to Sal and Mond; saw them reach the end of the beach and pause uncertainly.

Sal. Mond. Anything wrong?

There are no birds. It's too quiet, Sal said.

And a funny smell, Mond said.

All right. Stay there.

We'll go a little way. There might be Peeps.

No Peeps, Xantee's voice came, and Hari wondered again how she could hear everything.

Stay out of our heads, Xantee, Sal said angrily.

Sorry. But there's no Peeps. I'd feel them.

Well, we're going in to find out, Mond said.

Hari hesitated. He should stop them. But he liked these small disputes among the children to die naturally, not be settled by him, so he did not interfere. Sal and Mond were the most independent of the children. They were cousins who had come five years before from a nomadic tribe deep in the south. Although the other children had broken down most of their barriers against friendship there was a final boundary no one could cross, arising from an early life of riding on wide plains and herding goats and sitting quiet about the fire while the tribal bard sang rhyming songs of heroes fifty generations dead. Sal and Mond must be left to fit into the group in their own way. But they were sharp and quick, almost the equals of Xantee and Lo.

He watched them go into the scrub. There were no Peeps (the children's name for the people with no name); he trusted Xantee's judgement on that. But let the cousins find out for themselves.

Stop them before they go into the trees, though, Hari thought. They had said it was too quiet in the bush below the headland. No birds. And a strange smell. Hari did not like that. But Xantee had not smelled darkness. So, give Sal and Mond ten minutes, then call them back.

He let half the remaining children swim to the beach, with orders not to go near the scrub, and gave the others jobs about the vessel. If the scouting pairs reported no danger, he would spend the night anchored in this cove and sail on next morning, east a little way, charting the unknown coast, then north over five more days to home. I'll be there in time for harvest, Hari thought. And after harvest he and Pearl would take their holiday – take a small boat and sail wherever the winds took them.

Hari, Xantee's voice broke in. Something's wrong with Sal and Mond. Get there.

What?

Can't tell. Something they've never seen. They're afraid but I can't read them. There's a fog . . .

Tell them to get back.

I'm trying. They don't hear.

He saw Xantee burst from the scrub with Duro behind her and start running along the beach. At the eastern end Lo and Karl were running too – so Lo had heard.

Stay here, Hari ordered the children on the schooner. He dived over the side and swam to the beach. Back, he ordered the others. Karl, get them on board. Take charge.

Xantee and Duro were ahead of him. He ran, trying to come up with them.

Xantee, what do you hear?

Nothing.

Join with Lo.

There was a little explosion of concentrated effort, yet full of ease, as the pair wove themselves together.

Yes, we've got them. We can hear . . .

What?

Terror. Something's caught them. Something's sucking them in.

What is it?

We can't tell. It's got . . . Hari, it's got no being. It's something that can't be here. It can't exist.

It's here if it's got them, Hari said.

It's pulling them in. Hari, run.

He came up with Xantee and Duro as they reached the scrub.

Duro, come with me. Xantee, wait for Lo then come in together. Hold this thing back if you can.

He drew his black-bladed Dweller knife – forged for him in the north, a twin of the one his father had found in Blood Burrow – and went into the scrub with Duro pressing at his back. There was no time for caution. Now that he was close he could hear Sal and Mond for himself: little broken whimpers of terror and lost will. There was a smell too, like a fly-blown sheep.

The scrub ended. The jungle stood like a wall, with the headland rearing beyond. Everything looked normal. Yet this thing . . . Hari felt it plucking at him, slowing his blood in one part and making it rush in another, and slowing his mind.

Get out, he screamed, hurling all his strength against it – and felt it lurch with the shock of his blow, and then regather and try to wrap its mind around him. All right, he thought, if it's using its strength on me it can't be holding Sal and Mond.

He ran forward, plunging into spaces between trees, until the rocks of the headland were frowning over him. Sal and Mond lay in a clearing with close-packed trunks on three sides and a wall of stone at the back. They were locked in each other's arms like sleeping children, and they made no sound, neither cries nor whimpers nor the noiseless sound of speaking minds. They moved – moved – not of their own volition but with the motion of something pulled along by a rope. But nothing was there, nothing to pull them. There were only trees, the rock wall, with – now Hari saw – a litter of bones at its base. Sal and Mond inched towards that yellow cross-stitching of ribs and thigh-bones. Their progress was marked by a groove in the jungle floor.

Stay back, Duro, Hari said. His mind was working quickly. The base of the stone wall was the killing ground. Whatever had caught Sal and Mond lay there. It was almost invisible, a shimmer, and Xantee was right that it had no being – yet it could put out nets and lines like a fisherman and reel things in. He felt a wet rope snake around his leg, tugging him, but not with any strength, and he thought: It's only got enough for Sal and Mond, not for me at the same time; and hanging on to his image of fisherman and line, he slashed with his knife at the invisible rope holding him and felt something thicken against the blade, then part and fall away from his leg. He heard a sound – felt it rather, like the scratching of a thorn across his skin – a sound of pain as the thing retracted its line; and saw it for a moment as the pain forced it to drop its shield of invisibility – a gaping mouth, a blank disc-like eye, a straining bulk, bear-sized but jellyfish grey. Sal and Mond jerked forward as the shield came back. The thing pulled with urgency now, trying to get them in range of its mouth – inside its boat, Hari thought, hanging on to his image of a fisherman. The beast he had glimpsed was too outlandish to be real.

Xantee and Lo, in the trees, screamed in his head: Stay back, Hari.

He ignored them, while shouting at Duro: Grab their arms. Pull them.

He jumped forward and slashed at the place where the ropes or nets that held the cousins must be – the place beyond their outstretched legs. He felt the thickening, more resistant now, trying to blunt his knife, but the Dweller steel held its edge, and the ropes parted. Duro had Sal and Mond, one by an arm, the other by a plait of hair, and was dragging them back along the groove they had made.

Hari heard a hissing, like a snake, and jumped aside as something – arm, rope, tentacle – whistled past his head. He threw himself backwards, rolling in the air to land on his feet – Blood Burrow tactics – but the thing was quicker and he felt wet ropes, smoother than hemp, colder than winter streams, fasten round his legs, round his knife-arm and his throat. Something invaded him – not pain, no pain from the contact – a sickness, a nausea signalling appetite or pleasure in the creature that held him.

Pearl, he thought, we can't fight this.

As his consciousness seeped away he heard its mewing of hunger and greed. But heard too, far off, the voice of his children, Xantee and Lo, wrapping him round, gathering strength, loosening the ropes that held him, holding the creature still, although it raged and lurched and somersaulted its energies into new shapes – Xantee and Lo forcing it back, thinning its being, pushing it into its own space; and he felt, far away, Duro's hands on his ankles, pulling him out of the killing ground.

TWO

Duro hauled Hari like a sledge on to the beach. Xantee and Lo followed, each dragging one of the cousins. They had called Karl on the schooner and he and two of the children were waiting with canoes. They lifted Hari and Sal and Mond into the craft and set off. Duro swam with them. Xantee and Lo ran along the beach.

What was it? Where does it come from? Lo said.

Somewhere else. We've pushed it back but it'll come out again.

Will Hari be all right?

Don't know.

She thought of the marks the creature had left on his legs and throat, and the marks on the cousins' legs – grey, not red like abrasions, and cold when she laid her hand on them. Her palm was still numb from the touch and she stopped and scrubbed it on the sand.

Lo, help me.

They concentrated on her palm, calling blood into it, and in a moment something slid off like a film of ice. They saw where it fell by a shifting of sand grains.

It's alive.

It'll die.

She felt it die and caught a whiff of foul air.

Karl, she called, don't let anyone touch Hari's wounds. Or Sal's and Mond's. Be careful when you lift them.

They ran until they were opposite the schooner, then swam out. Already the children on board were hoisting sails. Xantee and Lo reached the side as the canoes arrived and Xantee repeated her warning – no touching the grey weals on Hari's and the cousins' skin.

How do we treat them? Duro said.

We fight them with our minds, round the clock, in teams. Maybe we can get them to slide off. It's the one on Hari's throat I don't like.

Could it stop him breathing?

We won't let it. I'll be with him all the time, or Lo when it's not me. Karl, get the crew moving. We'll get as far away from here as we can.

They put Hari in his cabin and Sal and Mond in the sick-bay. Karl soon had the schooner speeding across wind, away from the coast. Looking back, Xantee saw not a fog, not even a mist, but a dome of coldness over the jungle at the base of the headland. It had not been there when they sailed in. The creature had kept itself concealed.

She went to Hari's cabin and sat with him. His wounds – the weals on his skin – were unchanged and it made her shiver to think that they were not marks in his flesh but live bits of the creature from the jungle. She concentrated on them and felt she could hold them still, and stop them from feeding, if that's what they did – stop them from killing her father.

She sensed Lo at her side.

How are Sal and Mond?

Holding each other. We can't get them apart.

Don't try. Let them sleep. Just tell whoever's with them to make sure those marks on their legs don't grow. Help me with Hari.

They stood beside his bunk, holding hands. Hari lay on his back. His skin was bloodless under its natural brown and cold to touch, though covered with a sheen of sweat. Only the slight rise and fall of his chest showed he was alive.

We'll leave the marks on his arms and legs. Try to get this one off his throat.

It's deeper than the others, Lo said.

That thing must have known it had got him where it could kill.

How do we do it?

Go inside him. Bring as much warmth as we can. Bring his own blood into his throat. Make it melt this thing off.

They joined with the same effortless twining of minds they had discovered as they moved out of infancy. They did not make a single mind but two minds holding hands, or, as they sometimes thought of it, two containers touching at the brim, each pouring whatever it held into the other, while retaining the whole of itself. They felt it, simply, as a doubling of strength and knowledge, and an increase in quickness like the leaping of a deer.

Gently, with reverence – Hari was their father, who, with Pearl, they loved above all things – they invaded the inert shape on the bunk, avoiding his mind, finding the coldness wrapped about his throat. They probed at it, banged on it, but it gave no sign of life. It seemed to be resting, not increasing its hold, but lying embedded in Hari's throat like an iron torc. The tapping of Xantee's and Lo's minds made no more impression on it than a fingernail.

We can't shift it, Lo said.

Feel that? It's moving again. Lo, it's going deeper. I don't think we can make it let go but we've got to hold it. It'll kill him if it burrows in.

They fought against the creature – the fragment of a creature – for the next hour, holding it when it tried to hook itself deeper into Hari, when it tried to tighten like a noose and strangle him. They held it more easily than they had expected but could not make it give up even a small part of its hold.

I think it's stopping.

It has to rest. Lo, we can't keep this up forever. We've got to get him home fast and let the twins try. Tell Karl to put on all the sail he can. I'll get these other things off Hari's arms and legs.

She smelled the odour of exhaustion from the thing round Hari's neck, and with it, even stronger, the smell of rage and fear. Whatever it was feared her and Lo – but that gave Xantee little comfort. The creature might be alive, but it was only a fragment of something larger, even though it seemed to have a splinter of consciousness; and small or not, it threatened Hari's life. As for its mother – was that how to think of it? – the beast in the jungle, invisible on its pile of bones, where was it from, what was its nature? And was nature the right word? She could not forget the flash of understanding that had come to her when she felt its presence for the first time: this creature doesn't belong.

She concentrated, pulled all her strength into one spot and held it firm, and soon the grey infection – grey sore – she was attacking began to curl at the edges. It slid off Hari's ankle, melted in an instant, and was gone, leaving the stench of rotting flesh in the cabin.

Xantee held her breath, feeling dizzy, then felt an ugly tugging at the edge of her mind, and realised that the band on Hari's throat was at work again, hooking itself deeper into him, cell by cell.

Lo, she cried, and brought him running. They worked together again and held it still but could not make it weaken its grip. When it rested they rested. When it pushed again, trying to get deeper into Hari, they were ready and held it back. Duro and Karl came to help but the added strength made no difference. Xantee sent them to Sal and Mond's sickroom; where, working with teams of children, they were able to free the cousins from the fragments of the creature clinging to them.

But we can't make them let each other go, Karl said.

Leave them. They're keeping warm, Xantee said.

She was exhausted. She and Lo took turns sleeping on a cot at the foot of Hari's bed. The creature rested often, as though set by a clock. They knew when it would wake and sleep and although one of them always sat with Hari, holding his hand, feeding strength into him, the other was able to rest without the fear of a sudden attack.

Xantee dreamed, but it was the dreaming of recollection not fantasy. In the four days it took the schooner to cross the south-western arm of the Inland Sea, she relived her childhood, piece by piece, and understood, each time she woke, that her mind was reinforcing her, adding a layer to her consciousness and – this made her frightened – preparing her. For what? But she did not let fear get in the way of her delight in the reliving of her life, with its colours brighter and images sharper and its happiness more intense than she had been aware of at the time.

Pearl and Hari and Xantee, then Pearl and Hari and Xantee and Lo: a family. Later on, like new springs in the forest flowing down to join the larger one, came Blossom and Hubert. Six of us joined, said the dream that relived her life.

They lived in a timber house above a white-sand beach, with fields and gardens running back to the forest and a village growing beside them. Dwellers brought new children, some alone (orphaned in the wars), some with their parents, and all of them able to 'speak', faintly or well. First came Tealeaf, bringing Duro and his mother Tilly. Xantee was still in her cot but she remembered it – the dream remembered: the weariness of the travellers, their joy in arriving, and the small boy strapped on his mother's back, looking about him with inquisitive eyes. Xantee, she introduced herself, although she could not speak yet with her tongue. Duro, he replied. She had bonded with him almost as deeply as with her parents.

He had lost his father in a battle between the workers and the clerks, fought back and forth in the ruined streets of the city, Belong, and in Ceebeedee, and in a part of himself Duro knew of the loss and joined his mother in her grief, which seemed to deepen him, and slow him too, so that he was like a pool in a fast-flowing river, where the water pauses and the bottom falls away. He kept a larger part of himself secret than the other children, but was an adventurous and confident boy. Xantee came to love him almost as a brother yet was glad he remained strange in a way her real brothers did not. The dream seemed to say that the strangeness foretold another sort of love, but then it drew the knowledge quietly away.

Xantee slept. Swimming, running, climbing trees; learning to cook, learning to clean house; always learning – how to take a share of honey from the bees without being stung, how to plant seeds, how to winnow wheat, how to milk goats and how to shear them: the dream kept on. How to 'speak', although it needed little learning but came naturally. Learning to speak with her tongue, loud or soft, strident or sweet, was harder. She had not seen the need for it. But she discovered, after a time, that spoken words made a resting place, letting her mind sleep on the level that was otherwise so active; and, with those you loved, sound sometimes brought a greater intimacy. Sound, in many ways, went deeper than silence. She learned when to 'speak' and when to speak. And learned never to enter another person's mind without invitation, and learned the sinfulness of stealing memory, stealing time, of taking a mind away and moving it about as though pushing a bug with her fingernail. She could do that so easily – more easily than her mother Pearl or her father Hari. Yet she understood the sin. The lesson was to never do it, except . . . When was 'except'?

Xantee shivered in her sleep. There was danger from the

24

spitting snake, danger from the fangcat and tree tiger, and danger, when swimming, from the beakfish, whose mind was so small it was hard to find, and turning these creatures away was a matter of survival. But people must be left alone – unless they too became fangcat or tree tiger. Pearl and Hari had told Xantee and Lo, and later Blossom and Hubert, about Ottmar and Kyle-Ott, and Keech and the clerk who now called himself Clerk, and these men were more dangerous than beasts because their hunger was of the kind that could never be satisfied. As well as that, something spoke to them from the darkness, telling them they belonged there – a voice that Hari had also heard, and Pearl too, once, calling them into ways where they would consume other people. Whether dead Ottmar had understood, and Keech, still alive in the burrows, and the Clerk in the city; and whether they obeyed the voice or their own dark natures, Pearl and Hari did not know. Neither had ever heard the voice again, but heard the whisper that overcame it, saying their names – Pearl, Hari. And the children heard – Xantee, Lo, Blossom, Hubert – and could not imagine the darkness.

In her sleep, at the foot of Hari's bunk, while the creature from outside nature slept on her father's throat, Xantee dreamed the darkness and cried out, wailed and screamed, fearing that the dark voice would speak to her and she would not be able to resist. Lo calmed her. He told her to remember home. He sent pictures into her mind of the schooner cleaving through the sea and of Pearl, their mother, waiting on the shore. Then Xantee was able to dream happily again. When she woke she retained the darkness only as a shadow at the back of her mind.

The creature fastened on Hari's throat woke later in the day. They fought it and Hari lived.

We're close enough to tell Pearl what's happened, Xantee said.

Do you think we should?

You know how she and Hari are. They know everything about each other. I think I heard her whisper a while ago.

They combined their strength.

Pearl, they said.

She was waiting.

What's wrong? Is it Hari?

They hid nothing – the cousins, the invisible beast, Hari's fight with it, the living necklace strangling him.

Let me feel it, Pearl said.

They helped her and felt her mind recoil.

It's not from here, she whispered.

Where from?

The other side – I don't know. Can you hold it? Can you keep him alive? Once you're home the twins might be able to make it let go.

We can keep it from going deeper, that's all.

Put on more sail. Get here fast. Now make a path for me. Let me be with Hari for a while.

Xantee and Lo moved aside. They smoothed a way for their mother and kept their minds closed so she could speak with Hari alone – speak although he could not hear.

The cousins, Sal and Mond, looked in at the door. They were well again and moved freely about the schooner but no one could make them unlock their hands. Xantee and Lo thought they would hold hands for the rest of their lives.

Thank you, Hari, they said, and went away.

Xantee, Lo, Pearl said, it's waking up. I'll call the twins, they might be able to help you.

They heard her call Hubert and Blossom from the beach, where they were playing. At once their voices came through, clear, harmonious, but afraid.

What is this thing?

We don't know. It's awake. It's trying to burrow in. Help us.

Now, with four, and with the twins' strength, it was easier. Each time the creature tried to win a little more of Hari they saw it recoil, as though it felt the same horror for them they felt for it. Yet they could not make it let go. It was as if it had eaten and made parts of Hari part of itself, and could not regurgitate, though the pressure Hari's children exerted caused it pain so intense it mewed and wept. It was readier now to sleep and that gave Xantee time to wash Hari and change his bedding, and feed him, coaxing liquids down his constricted throat.

Four more days of sailing: the eastern hills came into sight.

Xantee, Lo, Pearl said, Tealeaf's coming. I've told her about Hari. She doesn't know what this thing is but she says there are legends.

There are always legends, Xantee said.

And we listen, Pearl said. Who knows where the answer lies?

Right. Meanwhile, this thing has got Hari in a vice. Maybe Tealeaf can tell us how to make it let go.

There might be some Dweller way, Pearl said.

And there mightn't, Lo said.

Well, the twins . . .

The twins were the best chance. Karl plied on more sail in

the morning breeze. All day the schooner sped towards the coast. As darkness fell the lights of the village pricked into life. Shyly, so as not to get in the way, the voices of children, two dozen or more, welcomed the travellers home – a chorus like birds waking in the dawn.

The schooner anchored at midnight. A dinghy was waiting. Karl and Duro lowered Hari into careful arms. The twins and Pearl were on the beach with a group of men holding lanterns. Others had a sprung cart to transport Hari to the farmhouse. Xantee and Lo felt the twins ease them aside from the task of keeping the creature on Hari's throat immobile. They were able to relax.

Pearl knelt beside Hari as Karl and Duro laid him on the cart. She stroked his face and spoke to him but no one heard what she said. Then she stood up and folded Xantee and Lo in her arms.

Thank you. If Hari had died . . .

He won't die, not now.

No. Go and sleep, Xantee. Sleep, Lo. We'll wake you if we need you.

She felt their exhaustion and touched her forehead to each of theirs.

Hari is lucky in his children.

They found their beds and slept the rest of the night and half the next day. Bleary-eyed, they ran down to the sea and swam out to the schooner and back, refreshing themselves. Hubert and Blossom joined them in the kitchen for lunch.

We've got this thing shut down, Hubert said. We've got it so if it moves or tries to go in deeper it gets a shock –

From us, Blossom said. Like from a battery. It just curls up.

It's scared of us.

But we can't make it let go. There's something making it hold on.

Maybe Tealeaf will know. How far away is she?

Nearly across. Another two days. Dweller boats are fast.

Have you two been up all night? Go and have a rest. Lo and I can help Pearl.

Call us, Blossom said, yawning.

So serious, Xantee thought, and they were only children, only nine years old. Brown-skinned, brown-haired, blue-eyed – they were as beautiful as forest animals, and as quick and instinctive, and to Xantee almost as strange, because their minds went places hers could not. She was a little jealous. She wished she and Lo had been twins. On the other hand, being free to take her mind privately wherever it wanted to go without having to shift someone out of the way – that was something she would not willingly give up. She wondered how free of each other the twins really were.

She took Pearl's place in the sickroom, made her rest, and felt the torc creature stir and then subside. She had been right, and the twins were right, it was afraid. And she had sensed fear in the beast in the jungle – the mother creature – when it felt Hari's strength, and hers and Lo's; yet it had only retreated as if to gather strength from a source behind it, in the rock wall, or perhaps deeper than that. She wondered if there were other creatures hidden there and they could unite the way she and Lo and the twins united. It was something she would ask Tealeaf when she came.

Xantee sponged Hari's brow. She dribbled cold water between his lips. Scar-faced Hari, she thought, Blood Burrow boy, knife-thrower, rat-killer (he had told them the tales), returner of the poison salt (but that was a tale made to be forgotten; the fewer people who knew about the salt the better), then Hari the farmer, Pearl's mate; and beautiful Pearl, Company woman, Radiant Pearl, Pearl Bowles – Xantee gave a little laugh. The tales led to her and Lo and Blossom and Hubert – and she wondered at the thousand chances of Hari and Pearl never meeting and there being no family on the farm by the Inland Sea; and, she thought, no one to fight this beast from outside nature living in our jungle, and living as a slimy band, sweating, pulsating, on Hari's throat. She touched it with a fingertip and felt its coldness and filth. Sniffed her finger, recoiled, and brushed the moist fragment off with her mind, smelled it dissolve.

Hari, she said, we'll make it let go. I promise we will.

THREE

Tealeaf and Pearl met on the beach and what they talked
about nobody knew. Tealeaf, the Dweller, with her three-
fingered hands and cat-pupilled eyes, had been Pearl's maid
in the city, in the days when Company had ruled. She had
opened Pearl out like folded paper and allowed the child to
become a woman, writing her own story on herself, instead
of the pretty painted object the men of Company preferred.
They had escaped from the city, meeting Hari in their
flight. Pearl and Hari had discovered ways of 'speaking' still
unknown to them. They had returned the poison salt to the
mine and buried it forever, and fallen in love . . .

Watching the two women on the beach, Xantee sighed.
What were they talking about as they strolled back and
forth? And how could they laugh, with Hari dying? Except
that he wasn't dying, Tealeaf knew that, he was just trapped
in the necklace and couldn't get free, and maybe Tealeaf was
teaching Pearl how they could help him and that was why

they laughed. Some Dweller way, or secret learned from the people with no name . . .

Her real name is Xantee, Xantee thought. I'm named after her.

She was jealous. She should be walking with the pair on the beach and learning their secrets. Tealeaf and Pearl were sharing the intimacy of sound, of words spoken aloud and laughter released into the air.

Tealeaf, Pearl, she murmured to herself.

Hush, Xantee, we're coming, Tealeaf said.

They walked up to the farmhouse and Xantee and Tealeaf hugged each other, and at once Xantee's jealousy fled, like a sickroom smell when a nurse throws open a window. She and Tealeaf had not met for more than a year, and if Tealeaf was eager to meet the others, especially the twins, and see Hari, she hid it, concentrating on Xantee, learning how she had grown and letting her feel the contours of her Dweller mind. Xantee knew other Dwellers but not one who had widened out into the world as Tealeaf had done, and learned the things Tealeaf knew. She was fascinated by the glimpses Tealeaf allowed of quiet places, wide seas, sunny weather, of people living in deserts or in the mountains or on ice floes, and the creatures they hunted. But at the back of each memory Xantee felt a storm, and behind every kindness cruelty lurked. Tealeaf's memories were a mixture of dark and light and the two would never be pulled apart. Xantee remembered her dream on the schooner and shivered, and Tealeaf said, speaking aloud, 'Don't try to know too much, Xantee. Wait and you'll understand.'

'But this thing,' Xantee said, 'that came out of the rock,

it's here, now. It's got my father.'

'Let's go and see him,' Tealeaf said.

They went into the sickroom, where Lo sat watching by the bed. Lo too knew Tealeaf's story and her part in Pearl and Hari's life. They met like old friends rather than woman and boy, but spent no time in greetings. The sight of Hari lying like a corpse on the bed was too much for Tealeaf. Tears sprang into her eyes.

'Hari, Hari.' She felt into his mind and found his will to stay alive, and wiped away her tears and said, This thing can't harm him any more. But how can we make it let go?

It does harm him, Pearl said. We can't feed him properly, he can't swallow. Water and broth and honey are the only things we can get down his throat.

The twins are out collecting honey now, Xantee said.

Tealeaf touched the necklace with her finger and drew back.

This is like nothing, she said.

But nothing that's just as real as what it feeds on, Pearl said.

It's lost, Tealeaf said, and it's alone. It wants to go back where it belongs.

Are you saying we should be sorry for it? Xantee said.

That would be pointless. This thing can only feed and destroy. And all we can do is destroy it in turn. There's no other way when something comes from outside nature.

So I was right, Xantee said. Outside nature.

I can't explain it any other way.

What do we do?

We keep him alive. Beyond that, I don't know.

The twins arrived from the forest carrying buckets of

33

honey. They put them in the kitchen and ran down to the beach to wash the stickiness off themselves.

They should have said hello to you, Xantee said.

Oh, I know the twins, Tealeaf said. We often talk.

Xantee felt foolish. Of course they did: the Dweller woman who was the strongest speaker of her kind, and the children who could work their speech past any barrier.

She took her turn sitting with Hari, while the others, Tealeaf and Pearl, and Lo and Blossom and Hubert, sat in the garden. If she wanted she could join her mind with theirs and hear what they said, but she preferred to be alone. She studied the necklace, the torc, on Hari's throat. Its colour, she imagined, was that of the lead suits the men who handled the poison salt had worn all those years ago in Deep Salt – the men Hari's father had called ghosts. Ghosts were outside nature too. Xantee shivered. She felt the cold radiating from the necklace, even as it slept. It had whitish veins in its flesh – if it was flesh – and they made little starts and jerks like her own pulse, sending some fluid perhaps, something that worked like blood, around the necklace keeping it nourished. When you looked at it like that, like an animal, it was almost possible to feel sorry for it, cut off from its mother and only wanting to stay alive. Was that what it wanted – to stay alive? Was it alive in any way she would recognise? And maybe life for it – and for its mother – meant simply destroying whatever it found on this side of the divide that kept it outside nature. Xantee was puzzled. I wish Tealeaf would explain, she thought.

She had a sudden longing not to be tangled in this way – not to be sewn into family but to roam free, the way Duro did. Since the age of fourteen, Duro had formed the habit of slipping away, of sometimes putting a whole mountain range between him and the village, so no one could call him – although, Xantee thought, the twins could make him hear if they tried, and I could too, because . . . She thought about it, as she had often done, enjoying the knowledge that he was open to her in a way he was not to anyone else, but asking now what that openness meant. And the access to her private thoughts she allowed him, was that any more than friendly trust?

I don't want to know yet, she thought. She drew back a little, brightened herself, and let her mind find Duro, working in the gardens.

What are you doing?

Digging bloody potatoes, Duro said. It's killing my back. How's Hari?

The same. Who's there?

Karl. I can't keep up with him. Sal and Mond, working with one hand each. They're going to be useless from now on.

Give them time.

I'd sooner give them a kick up the arse. What did they go close to that thing for?

They didn't see it. Tealeaf's here, Duro. Are you and Tilly coming to see her?

Tonight.

I don't think Tealeaf knows what that thing in the jungle is.

She's got to. Otherwise we can't get Hari free.

We will. I know we will. Can you come swimming when I'm finished here?

If I get another row dug. Bloody potatoes.

She said goodbye and concentrated her attention on the

necklace, trying to read it, trying to find if it had a brain. It must have – some fragment of the larger creature's brain – to give it the cunning for its sudden attacks. It knew fear too, so it was more than a plant. What was it and where did it come from? Tealeaf must know.

She swam with Duro late in the afternoon. The twins and then Lo and Pearl sat with Hari, while Tealeaf visited Tilly, Duro's mother, who had helped her and Pearl escape from the city in the time of Company.

That night, after a meal in the farmhouse kitchen, they sat on the porch overlooking the bay and Tealeaf told them what was happening out in the world – in the lands over the western ocean, in the southern lands and in the city. Most of it was an old story to Xantee and Lo. They knew there was no word from the west, that there had been no word for many years. No travellers came, no fugitives from the broken empire of Company. And south and east little kingdoms, no more than fortified villages, and little kings, no more than bandit chieftains, had sprung up. They fought, they raided, and some prospered for a while. No man or woman had appeared strong enough to unite them. As for the mass of the people, they lived from hand to mouth. They tilled a few sparse fields and brought in crops if the bandits allowed. They survived from season to season, or they died.

But the Clerk is really a king, isn't he? Lo said. He's got a proper army and he rules over City and the old factory towns.

He pretends to rule. But there's no peace, always rebellion – and murder and starvation and slavery. He sits in Ceebeedee, what's left of it, and tries to believe he's in control.

But Keech won't let him, Duro said.

No, Keech won't. He's buried as deep in the burrows as the Clerk is in Ceebeedee. They keep on making pacts and breaking them and murdering each other's messengers. Keech goes out and raids the caravans bringing food to the city. The Clerk poisons the wells Keech gets his water from. Then they make another treaty, and break it. They say you can see hatred drifting back and forth like a mist, from the burrows into the city and from the city back into the burrows. Then Keech and the Clerk meet to talk terms – they meet on the hill, by Ottmar's mansion – and they make a new agreement and you see their hands twitching with their eagerness to strangle each other.

But all this doesn't matter, Pearl said.

It matters to the children who are starving and the people in the burrows dying every day – in the city too – while these tyrants swell and contract like sucker toads on a dead mudfish, Tealeaf said.

They had not often heard her speak so bitterly. Dwellers were calm by nature. Calmness was like a sense with them – but Tealeaf had seen too much pain and misery. She gave herself a shake – a mental shake – and settled down.

But I know what you mean, Pearl.

There's this new thing now. It will kill us all, Pearl said.

Yes, it will.

And nobody knows what it is?

Nobody knows. The one Hari fought isn't the first.

There are others? You've seen others?

No. I've heard of them.

She told them that the people with no name had found

37

them first: tiny creatures, no bigger than slugs, oozing from damp crevices low on seamed hillsides, or surfacing in the red water of swamps. They hid in the roots of drowned trees and under slabs of moss in the mouths of caves, not many of them, twenty or thirty perhaps, in the hills and jungles east of City, but the people with no name, who knew everything old and everything new in their ancient lands, sensed them at once. They wove harmonies around them and held them like flies trapped in a web, so the creatures could neither retreat nor grow. They struggled, unable to live, unwilling to die, making a tiny mewling like starved cats, below the threshold of human hearing, almost below that of the people with no name. And those ones, the first, were still there.

The people – you call them Peeps, Tealeaf said, and I don't think they'd like it if they found out – the people try to send them back where they came from, but they can't, there's no way back, just an immense will in these creatures to break free. To devour and grow.

When did it start? Duro said.

Seven or eight years ago.

And now . . . ?

The people can't be everywhere. They've got these things – they call them gools in their language and gool means unbelonger – they've got these infant gools tied up –

Infant?

The size of your fist. You've seen a larger one. How big?

It was invisible some of the time, or shimmering. But when we could see it – as big as a cave bear, Xantee said.

But there was more of it hidden in the rock, Duro said.

Yes, oozing through the rock, through veins and fissures

and underground streams a mile deep, and joined to others, and all reaching back to the place where it began, where there's something drinking up the life of the world. This creature has learned to find places where the people are not, where it won't be found. It's grown there patiently, in a dozen places, and now it's ready to break out. Sal and Mond found one. Hari too.

What is it? Xantee breathed.

I don't know. The people don't know. Something that follows its own nature. Something that will turn the world inside out. It will suck it dry of all its life and be the only life the world knows.

You said, Xantee began. She was terrified and had to swallow before she could go on. You said 'back to the place it began'. Do the Peeps know where that is?

They don't leave the jungle so they can't trace it further than the jungle's edge. But they point – they point us with their minds – towards the city. They hear something there. They feel it and they're afraid. In all the time Dwellers have known them, the people have never been afraid.

What do they hear?

They can't say. It's the sound of something growing. The sound of something sucking and getting stronger – but they're confused because it doesn't seem to fill any space. It always seems to be on the other side of what it's feeding on.

In the city? Xantee said. Is it in the burrows or on the hill?

And what does it feed on? Duro said.

People. Animals. Trees. The stone itself. You find hillsides crumbled into dust, with all the things that held them together sucked out. But no sign of the creature.

We saw one, Xantee said. There's part of it tied round Hari's neck.

The one you found is the furthest from the city we've heard of. But somewhere in the city, or in the burrows, or on the hill, there's the thing that breeds them. The mother of the thing that's choking Hari.

So it's there? Xantee whispered. In the city? Why doesn't it swallow the city up?

Because we think somehow the city is its home. It's the place where it was born. Or the gate it can come through. It's where it rolls over and comes out of nothing into something.

And then it puts its arms out . . . Duro began.

Underground. Along the sunken rivers, until it finds a new place to break out . . .

Nobody spoke. They were too afraid. The sun was sinking like a stone, colouring the clouds blood red and deepening the Inland Sea until it seemed like a hole. The twins were sitting one on each side of Pearl. She put her arms around them.

This thing on Hari's neck . . . ?

Is part of it, Tealeaf said.

And it will never let go?

I don't think it can.

So in the end he'll die.

No he won't, the twins said in unison. We won't let him.

He'll waste away, Pearl said. We can't get enough food into him.

The thing will die, Tealeaf said, when its mother dies.

Can anyone kill her?

I don't think so.

Let us try, said the twins.

40

No, said Pearl.

Let Lo and me, Xantee said.

No.

First we'd have to find out where she lives . . .

No, I said. It's too dangerous for children.

We're not children. We're as old as you and Hari were when you stole the salt and stopped Ottmar.

I'll go with them, Duro said.

Listen, Tealeaf said. There's a tale –

Always a tale, Duro grumbled.

It's not a Dweller story, it's a human one, from over the jungles and plains, in the fishing towns on the eastern coast. And it comes across the centuries, because the towns are no longer there, nor are the people who lived in them, they migrated eastwards in their boats a thousand years ago –

But left their stories behind, Duro said.

Yes, Duro, Tealeaf smiled. But listen and you might learn.

It was the tale of a man called Barni, a fisherman, and of a beast that lived in a cave on the rocky shore and came out at night to swallow vessels venturing too close. It was a grey creature, bulbous, one-eyed, insatiable, and sometimes it could be seen and at other times not. The villagers tried to catch it in their nets. It swallowed the nets, and grew. They tried to burn it. It swallowed the fire. Spears did not harm it. It did not bleed. Its arms stretched out into the sea and up the cliffs. It ate every living creature and grew and grew.

It's the thing we found, Lo whispered.

Perhaps, Tealeaf said.

The villagers fought it and, one by one, the beast captured and devoured them. Barni was the only one who did not fight. He watched the creature. How had it been born? Where had it come from? He remembered the time when village children played in the cave. In those days two new stars appeared in the sky, a white one in the north and a red in the south, each with a tail shaped like a skinning knife. They brought great storms that smashed the jetties and blew the roofs off houses. The people made sacrifices to their gods. They prayed to them but the gods did not listen and the stars remained, white in the north, red in the south. They seemed to hiss and spit at each other. The storms blew and more boats were lost, but life went on, until two children playing in the cave on the shoreline vanished as if it had swallowed them. Their parents searched and they too vanished, but the next tide rolled their skulls out of the cave like pumpkin shells. The beast had arrived.

Barni thought about it. The creature ate and grew, it excreted foul liquids, it puffed out grey dust. Sometimes it rested. Sometimes when men crept in to fight it, it oozed back into the walls and slept.

Why does it sleep? When does it sleep? he asked himself.

He made a chart, his beast-chart, and studied it and the answer came: It sleeps on the nights when black clouds pile up in the sky and blot out the red star and the white.

He went to the village council and told them what he had found.

The elders grew angry with him. Everyone knew it, they said – although they had not mentioned it themselves. It was no help. What must they do?

Barni had the answer: We must build a ship with great sails to catch the storm, and sail it into the sky, with strong men armed with spears, and slay the red star and the white. Then the beast will sleep forever.

That's impossible, Duro said.

It's a tale, Duro. It's a myth, Xantee said. Listen.

Tealeaf went on: So they built a ship larger than any ever seen before, with great square sails to catch the wind, and when the next storm blew, the men of the village went on board with their spears, and Barni took the tiller and they sailed out into the eastern sea. The sails puffed out like bladder fish and the great ship climbed into the sky.

Impossible, Duro growled.

They approached the white star and the first squad of men threw their spears and the star gave a cry like a wounded bear, and blazed red and then grew pale and died. Barni thrust the tiller round and the ship sailed south, through the gathering clouds, to the red star –

And the second squad of men threw their spears, Duro said.

Quiet, Xantee said. She reached out and held his hand.

The men threw. The spears flocked down like hawks swooping on their prey, and pierced the star, which gave a shuddering cry, like an old man dying, and shed its light into the black sky –

And down in the cave the beast died, Duro said. Crap.

Ah, Duro, Tealeaf said, if you would only open your mind a little. But yes, the beast died. It howled and hissed and writhed and shrank and thinned its flesh until there was no flesh left, but a foul-smelling mist, which twisted like smoke out of the cave, and the storm turned in its tracks and blew it away. That's the story. You can take it any way you like.

So they made Barni their king, Lo said.

No, it's not that sort of tale. He went back to being a fisherman, and grew old and died too, many hundreds of years ago. It's better to be part of a story than be a king.

It means, Pearl said.

Yes, Pearl, what does it mean?

That the beast Sal and Mond found isn't the first. There've been others, centuries ago, and it means . . .

What?

There are ways to kill them.

What ways? Xantee said.

You build a ship and sail it to the stars, Duro said, grinning when Xantee squeezed his hand angrily. He had seen the point of the story.

It means, I think, Tealeaf said slowly, that there are only a few times when this creature can be born. The conditions have to be right – there has to be a red star and a white.

What are they? Xantee said.

I've no idea.

This Barni was human, not a Dweller?

Yes, human. Listen to me.

She seemed older suddenly, with her cat eyes faded and her three-fingered hands bonier. She's seen too much, she's learned too much, Xantee thought. And Tealeaf read it.

No, Xantee, she said, it isn't what I know, which is far from being enough. It's what I'm not able to do. Dwellers work differently from humans. Our minds travel in different ways. I can understand this story of Barni and the stars but I can't see what to do about it.

She shook her head. That will be for humans to work out.

Us, Xantee said.

Work it out first, then do something about it, Duro said. What were those fishermen called, Barni's people?

I've heard them called Wideners, because they sailed away from the coast, across the ocean. Others simply called them the Fish People.

And they're gone?

The storms were too much for them. The eastern coast was too barren. They heard of calmer seas and flatter shores across the Great Sea. So they migrated. You can still find their traces, people say. Ruined villages. A few broken sea walls around their tiny harbours. That's all.

No use going there, then, Duro said.

But there must be records. Or histories. It can't all be lost, Xantee said.

If we can find out what the stars really were . . . Duro said.

A cry came from the sickroom. Tilly, who was not a 'speaker', was sitting with Hari. Pearl ran inside, with the twins following. A moment later Tilly came out, her face pale and strained. She sat by Duro, who put his arm around her.

'Easy, Ma.'

'It started to wake up. It started turning over inside its skin.'

'Pearl's there now.'

'I can't bear looking at it. It's eating Hari.'

'We've got it like a rat in a trap,' Duro said. 'It's got no chance.'

'But you can't kill it. And Hari can't stay like that.'

They knew it was true, and sat brooding, while dull red sunset streaks faded from the sky. Tealeaf closed her eyes and rocked back and forth.

She's growing old, Xantee thought.

If Tealeaf picked up the thought, she did not respond.

There were tales, she said. Then she deepened her eyes and spoke aloud so Tilly would also hear: 'There were tales –'

Not more of them? Duro said.

Shut up, Duro, Xantee said.

'Not myths, just bits of knowledge Dwellers picked up about the city when it was called Belong. It was a great city and a great civilisation, but growing fat and lazy, and easy prey for Company when its ships arrived. Hari's people lived there, the Belongers.'

'He's told us about it,' Lo said.

'And about Blood Burrow,' Xantee said.

'Yes, Blood Burrow. And Keech Burrow, and Keg and Bawdhouse. All the burrows. And Port. And the old man, Lo the Survivor – you're named after him, Lo.'

'Yes, I know.'

'Hari told me that Lo talked about great galleries and concert halls his father's father had seen when he was a child. And a library where all human knowledge was stored. The stories – the histories – of all the races the Belongers had ever met. But everything, the storerooms and stacks, were buried in the rubble when Company's fleet came back after the rebellion and broke Belong into little pieces with its bolt cannons. Ten days and nights they stood off shore, turning the city into broken walls and buried rooms . . .'

'Hari used to cry when he told us,' Xantee said.

'That's when the burrows were born. Company kept it that way – rubble and swamps and pits and hovels – so the Belongers would never have the strength to rebel again. Hari was born there. No wonder he cried.'

'He never told us about libraries,' Xantee said. 'I'm not sure what they are. Books and things?'

'Lo the Survivor told him about them. Hari never found them. He wouldn't have known what a book was if he'd picked one up.'

'So even if we could talk to him . . .'

'He couldn't tell you where to go. But there is someone you can talk to. Someone who knows the burrows even better than Hari. If you can find him.'

'Who?'

'Tarl, Hari's father.'

'The Dog King,' Xantee said.

'We don't even know if he's still alive,' Duro said.

'He's alive. The people with no name know where he is.'

'Can we go to him? Duro and me? And get him to guide us?'

'And me,' Lo said. 'I'm going.'

'And us,' said the twins.

'No, not you. You've got to stop here and keep Hari alive until . . .' Tealeaf stopped.

'Until Tarl takes us to the city,' Xantee whispered. 'And we find out what the stars were. And the gool. And how to kill it.'

She felt small and weak, which confused her. All her life she had been certain nothing would prove too much for her. But now, looking at her fingers, skin and bone, she saw how fragile they were; and looking into her mind, which had seemed limitless, she felt she might break out the other side and find nothing – nothing but the beast opening its black mouth at her.

Duro held her hand.

She swallowed.

Tealeaf, she said in Tealeaf's mind, *you'll have to persuade Pearl. She won't let us go.*

She will. She'll understand there's no other way. You're children of the burrows, like Hari. And you, Duro, a child of the city. You were born for this.

FOUR

The sea was calm for two days, then a storm blew up from the south, making waves with jagged tops that struck the schooner sideways and seemed to want to bite her in two. Karl found shelter in a cove, where they lay for a night and a day, Xantee fretting at the lost time and talking back through the storm to the twins at home: How was Hari?

No better, no worse, they said. The necklace had hardened into an iron band and seemed to be in a kind of hibernation. But water, milk, honey, broth, would not keep Hari alive forever.

Tealeaf was on the schooner guiding them to a river on the south-eastern shore, where they might find the people with no name. She kept Xantee busy with tasks about the boat and in the galley, or sat talking with her, telling stories of her life in the city, when she had been Pearl's maid.

Three hours dressing for a ball? Xantee said. It was hard to believe.

And another hour painting her face. And two hours for her hair, with maids weaving pearls into the braids, so a man called Ottmar might notice her.

That's Ottmar the king, who was killed by the dogs?

By Tarl's dogs. Tarl learned how to talk with dogs.

And he told them to kill Ottmar?

They were cruel days, Xantee. They're cruel days still. Nothing changes.

And Tarl still talks with dogs? Will we find him?

I think so. Whether he'll help you is another matter.

The storm died away and the schooner sped south. Mountains towered like thunder clouds on the third day, and on the fourth Xantee saw black jungles sweeping down to the shore, streaked with red from summer trees flowering in gullies. She wondered if gools had come this far. There were bitten cliffs where seams of dampness might break out. She tried to sense the dome of coldness that had hung over the gool Sal and Mond had found, but only the shimmer of heat and dampness lay on the jungle.

Lo, she called, and he came from his job reading the wind for Karl at the tiller.

Can you feel anything? Has it come here?

They sent their minds out in unison, but in the heat and steaminess found no prickle of cold.

It's a big world and this thing's small, Lo said.

But it's growing.

Yet the size of the mountains and the sea comforted Xantee. Then she remembered the living torc back home, that tiny bit of the creature locked on Hari's throat. They must find where it had been born, and kill whatever lived there.

She felt sick with fright, at the thing itself, and what she and Lo and Duro must do.

One step at a time, Duro said, from his job trimming sails.

Who invited you in? Xantee said.

When you're squealing everyone hears, Duro said.

I don't squeal.

You squeak.

I do not.

Lo laughed. Tealeaf says we'll anchor by this river of hers tonight. See if you can stop squabbling by then.

He went back to Karl.

Xantee shut her mind to Duro. But she was pleased by his intrusion. She knew he thought she was conceited, that she thought herself more gifted than the others, and he had ways of making her see how ordinary in most things she was – in generosity (she was inclined to greediness and selfishness), in looks (she was no beauty, not alongside her mother, Pearl), in strength (no match for Duro), in voice (yes, she was inclined to squeal and squeak). Duro made her see it, but let her see he liked her anyway. Xantee laughed. Well, she thought, aren't I perfect in everything else? She heard Duro laughing too. How had he got back in?

They anchored off the river mouth as the sun went down. The jungle blackened in an instant and the cries of night animals rose – shrieks, warbles, long melancholy fading shouts that seemed almost human.

Do the Peeps know we're here? Lo said.

They know, Tealeaf said. We'll go ashore in the morning and talk to them.

Can I talk? Xantee said.

If they let you.

How many are going on this expedition? Karl said.

Just three. Xantee and Lo and Duro. Not you, Karl. You have to sail the boat back home.

We want to go, Sal and Mond said with one voice.

No, Tealeaf said.

Although they had worked hard on the boat, the cousins made only one set of hands. Sal's right was locked in Mond's left and never let go. Sleeping, eating, washing, working, Sal and Mond were one; and the locking was mental as well as physical. They found little need to speak with other people. Their minds were closed.

They need to travel quickly and you'd slow them down, Tealeaf said.

The cousins turned away. They shifted to the schooner's bow and stared into the dark.

At midnight Xantee rose from her bunk. Heat rolled off the jungle, enveloping the little ship and seeping into its corners. She took a blanket, hoping to find a cooler place on deck.

Duro was already there, sleeping by the rail. She lay down by his side, trying not to wake him. He was breathing easily, but after a moment he gave a cry like a tree cat and woke with a start.

What? Xantee said.

You here? What's wrong?

It was too hot to sleep. Did you have a dream?

Bloody nightmare. I had a gool around my throat. They scare me, Xantee.

Me too. I just want to curl up. I want to be safe.

They held hands.

52

I'd get out of this if I could, Duro said.

So would I. But we can't.

No, we can't.

So . . . tomorrow.

Yes, tomorrow.

After a while they slept, but movements woke them before long. Sal and Mond came on deck. Each wore a pack, Sal's slung over her left shoulder, Mond's over her right.

We're leaving, Mond said.

Where? said Duro.

If we can't go hunting this gool with you we'll go by ourselves.

In the city?

Wherever we find it. It touched us, not you, so it's ours to kill.

It touched my father. It's killing him, Xantee said.

Hari saved us, Sal said, so when we find the gool we'll save him.

Have you heard the story of the two stars?

We don't need stories, Sal said.

We'll take a canoe and leave it at the river, Mond said.

How will you find your way after that?

We'll find it.

The jungle will kill you, Duro said.

If it does it does.

Xantee watched them lower a canoe over the side. They were quick and agile. Already they had learned ways of moving and compensating. In the dark she could not see their faces, but saw their eyes shine. Two girls, wiry, supple, smaller than northern people, quicker too, and braver and more ready to die. If only they weren't locked together they might stand a chance in the jungle. She wondered if, in the end, their joined hands would grow together and learn skills impossible for one.

Goodbye, she said.

They answered in their own language and paddled away, Mond with her arm angled back to Sal. That was not a new skill, Xantee thought, it was simply awkward.

They're dead, Duro said.

They tried to sleep again and managed an hour or two before dawn. As the first light showed, Xantee stood at the rail searching the river mouth for the cousins, but they were gone. Tealeaf came on deck and stood beside her.

I felt them go.

Will the Peeps help them?

Maybe. They're a bit like the people themselves.

By mid-morning Xantee and Lo and Duro were ready to leave. They took packs, like the cousins, and knives as weapons. They took all the lessons Hari and Pearl and Tealeaf had taught them: survival lessons, fighting lessons, speaking lessons, food-gathering lessons, stories of the city and the burrows, stories of the jungle and the people with no name, and of Tarl the Dog King and his black Dweller knife. They took their determination to save Hari, which was firm in each of their minds, but faltering and thin when they tried to imagine how it might be done.

Karl lowered a dinghy and rowed them to the river mouth, then up a broad reach close to the jungle, where tangled creepers screened the banks and trees with fat trunks and heavy branches and leaves the size of bucket lids squatted low.

The canoe Sal and Mond had taken lay on a mud bank joining the shore. Tealeaf probed the creepers for hidden water choppers – a single bite would take an arm or leg – but found none.

Sal and Mond's footprints, Lo said, pointing to ooze-filled puddles in the mud. They got into the trees all right.

I hope the Peeps have found them, Duro said.

The people have been here. I can smell them, Tealeaf said. Karl, come back for me at dark. We'll leave the canoe as a gift.

Karl rowed away, speaking cheerfully, sending them on their way, but they heard the hidden sadness in his voice. Karl did not believe they would come back.

The cousins' footprints led into the trees, then vanished. All around, the jungle hissed and moaned with hidden life.

What do we do now? Lo said.

Wait and listen, Tealeaf said. She stopped in a clearing.

There are no hunting animals, Xantee said. The Peeps don't need to protect us.

Pearl and Hari had told her how the people had helped them through the jungle on their flight from the city. They wove harmonies around them painful to the animals that would have taken them as prey. Pearl had been able to hear the protecting song but could not hear the people's voices when they spoke. Tealeaf could hear. Dwellers had centuries of knowledge of the people.

The afternoon was half gone when a whisper came. It said: Dweller. It said: Child.

Yes, I'm a Dweller, Tealeaf whispered. We've spoken before.

You are Xantee. Who is the child?

Xantee too. She is human.

And the other child?

Lo.

And the one who doesn't hear?

He's Duro. He can speak with us but not with you.

Two others came, hand in hand.

Their fear of the gool has locked them together. So they seek the gool to kill their fear. I did not know they would hear you.

There are few, the whisper said. Now let the children Xantee and Lo say what they want.

I'm not a child, Xantee said softly.

How many summers have you seen?

Fifteen.

A child then. And Lo is younger. The one who doesn't hear, how many summers?

Sixteen.

Xantee looked at Duro and saw him standing back from them, alert, not hearing what was said but ready for anything he must do.

He can't speak with you, but he stood on a hill last summer and heard the great voice say his name, she said.

Then he is one we'll help, whispered the Peep. Now tell us, Xantee, where you are going and what you will do.

First, who are you? Can we see you?

Every noise and movement fled away. The jungle held itself still. Xantee grew afraid. She felt Tealeaf's anger, and knew her questions broke some law. She sent her mind out, questing, but found emptiness all around. The Peeps were gone.

Stupid girl, Tealeaf said.

56

I didn't know.

The people won't be named. They won't be seen. It's against their nature.

But I saw a kind of flittering in the trees, like bits of light.

That's all you'll see. Now wait. They'll come back if they can.

And if they can't? Lo said.

Then you'll go on alone.

They helped Sal and Mond.

Sal and Mond knew not to ask questions.

Slowly the jungle sounds returned – moans and squeaks and slitherings and whispers – but no Peeps came. Xantee sat on her pack and brooded. Humans, Dwellers and Peeps were united against the gools. There was no time for stupidity, hers or the Peeps. Yet there were ancient laws her curiosity had infringed against, and it had caused pain. She had felt the stab of it as the Peeps fled.

I'm sorry, she whispered.

No answer. It was not until late in the day, when the gloom in the jungle clearing had deepened almost to night, that she felt a feather-light stroking on her mind.

Xantee?

I'm here.

Say what you want now, but ask nothing.

We want . . . She collected her thoughts and spoke carefully: We want to find the gool. My father fought with it and it wrapped a piece of itself round his neck. His name is Hari. Unless we find the place where it's born, and find a way to kill it, he'll die. And . . .

Yes, speak.

The gool is growing. Something hidden somewhere keeps it alive. We don't understand what. Or where it lives. Or how to fight it. But there are stories.

She told them the tale of the red star and the white.

So we're going to the city to find the meaning of the stars.

We know nothing of the city.

There's a man who does. He lived in the burrows. His name is Tarl, the Dog King. Hari is his son.

We know of Tarl.

So, what we want is for you to show us the way to him, that's all. And I'm sorry we call you Peeps. And I'm sorry that I hurt you.

Silence came again, but this time nothing fled. Xantee felt that the people were holding her apology up and turning it round to see what it was made of.

I mean it, she said. And I think we're on the same side.

Yes, we are. We have a pact with Dwellers. Now we make one with you. But reaching the Dog King isn't easy. He's far away. There are mountains to cross.

We want to go as fast as we can.

Then go. When first light comes, take the canoe the joined ones left. Follow the river two days to the place where it falls from the mountain. You'll find people waiting there to help you.

Thank you, Xantee said.

No answer came. The people with no name were gone.

Who are they? Xantee whispered.

No one knows, Tealeaf said. No one sees them. But Dwellers believe they're only half our size. They've got arms and legs, like us, and eyes and ears, and they eat and drink and sleep and wake, like us. They've been in the jungle forever and will be here when the world dies – that's what Dwellers say. What the people say, no one knows.

So let's not ask any questions, Duro said. Let's just go. This jungle's getting too dark for me.

They heard the rattle of Karl's oars on the river and his voice calling from the mud bank. Lo answered silently. Human sounds had no place among the animal cries increasing as the darkness increased. They made their way quickly to the river. Duro and Lo pulled the canoe to a drier part of the mud bank, making it safe. Then Tealeaf said goodbye, entering their minds one by one. She knew – they all knew – they might never meet again. She climbed into the dinghy and Karl rowed away. Soon the creak and splash of oars were all that was left. Further out, beyond the river mouth, faint yellow lights gleamed on the schooner. They seemed to be on another world. Near at hand a different sort of splashing sounded.

Chopper, Duro said.

But he can't get near us, Lo said. Hear the people.

Can they make sounds underwater? Duro said. Let's get back in the trees.

They returned to the clearing where they had spoken with the people and built a small fire and ate a meal. Then they laid out their sleeping mats and wrapped themselves in blankets – one thin blanket each in the hot night. There was no need to keep watch. Animals barked and hooted in the jungle but the singing of the people, almost too thin to be heard, kept them away. Xantee felt how ill-made she was – curious, pushy in the daytime, and with ears so dull in the night she could barely hear harmonies that tree tigers and fangcats heard so painfully. The sound kept biting insects away as well.

Thank you, she murmured. And keep bad things out of my dreams, if you can. And Lo's dreams. And Duro's dreams.

They were asleep already. She touched each one lightly on the face, and slept too.

FIVE

The waterfall curved like a skein of wool and shattered into spray on coal-black rocks at the river's end. It roared like volcanic steam, yet a rainbow hung across it as peaceful as a painting on a wall.

Paddling had been hard against the river's flow. Their sleep had been uneasy, without the people to protect them. One of them always had to stay awake. They could not set up harmonies to keep animals off, but several times joined their minds to push them away. The waterfall, impassable though it was, marked a new beginning. There would be Peeps to help and guide them on their way.

They camped at the edge of the spray, close enough to enjoy its cooling touch. No fire was possible, which increased the danger from animals – but presently a voice whispered: Xantee, Lo.

Yes. We thank you for your help, Xantee said.

You're safe here tonight. Follow us in the morning.

That was all, but after a moment the singing began, weaving through the clamour of the waterfall. Xantee tried to help Duro hear, and soon he was able to pick out a pleasant buzzing. Xantee, listening with him, heard a lilting and retreating and advance, like her mother Pearl playing her flute, and she wondered if one day humans would learn the people's music and travel through the jungle without help.

They slept well that night, but woke with their blankets and clothes sodden from drifting spray.

This is a place where there could be gools, Lo said.

The people would have told us, Xantee said.

No gools, whispered a voice.

Can you tell us if Sal and Mond – the two who are joined – came this way? Xantee asked.

No one has come.

They're not looking for the Dog King, Lo said. They're heading for the city. They'll be further west.

They ate wet food and drank cold water. Duro pulled the canoe under the trees as a gift for the people. The sun was playing rainbow colours across the waterfall when they started out. Now and then a whisper came, leading them eastwards through giant trees. They began to climb. By midday the trees were smaller and the understorey thinner, but at nightfall the jungle still enclosed them. Again they slept well, and Xantee, waking early, enjoyed the gleam of stars through the canopy. She had missed them in the deeper jungle.

At dawn the people roused them with a voice that seemed more distant: Now you must go on alone. Climb into the open slopes and then into the mountains. The pass lies between the fist and the serpent's head. Beyond there is jungle again, and higher mountains. The people will help you.

How far to the Dog King? Lo said.

We don't know. The Dog King is never in one place. Beyond the furthest mountains, that's all we know.

Are there any gools?

We know of one, far away. The people will take you safely past.

The knowledge that one of the beasts lay ahead, even though distant, struck cold into them. But when they had climbed for another hour and broken out of trees on to slopes of coarse grass and sliding stone and seen the jungle stretching behind them and the white line of the Inland Sea, and seen how big the world was and how it stretched out and seemed to yawn, Xantee felt her fear slip away. The gool could take only little bites.

Little bites are enough when it's got forever, Duro said.

I want to talk to Blossom and Hubert, Lo said. They mightn't be able to reach us over the mountains. I want to find how Hari is.

And Pearl, Xantee said. Her mother's fear and sadness had been with her, like a silent companion, ever since they had left the farm. The thought of her sitting by Hari, watching him waste away, caught her like a bone broken in her chest.

Let's climb first, Duro said. We'll try when we get to the pass.

At noon they reached the formations the people had told them of, one shaped like a hooded serpent ready to strike, the other like a clenched fist defying it. They sat in the cool sunlight and ate strips of dried meat and jungle fruit.

Now Xantee, Lo said, the twins.

They stood and faced the jungle and the Inland Sea and joined hands, joined minds, like two strands of wool weaving in and out, and Xantee understood, in her closeness to her brother, how Sal and Mond must feel – their need, after the terror they had known, and the living dead thing that had dragged them to its mouth, to stay with each other forever.

Yes, Lo whispered, agreeing.

They sent out their call: Blossom, Hubert – and in a moment their intertwined voices replied: Xantee, Lo, where are you?

In the mountains. We mightn't be able to speak from the other side.

But we'll reach you, and we can feel you, and we'll know . . .

They did not go on. They would know if Xantee and Lo died. They would feel it like a missed beat of the heart or a breath that could no longer be drawn.

How's Hari? Lo and Xantee said.

He doesn't change. We feed him honey and milk. Pearl washes him. She sings him songs and plays her flute to him. We can find a little bit of him not sleeping. He hears but he doesn't understand.

Is Pearl all right?

She's sleeping. She's been up all night, watching him, and watching the thing on his neck. Xantee, Lo, she'll die if he dies. Find the gool and kill it.

We will, they breathed.

And come back to us, because . . . you must.

They heard the childishness of the command, and

answered with a confidence they did not feel. Then Duro sent a message for the twins to tell his mother: Hi Ma. Go easy on those pancakes. Save some for me. And here's a kiss.

Their talking was done. Painfully – it was always painful – they unclasped their minds, envying the twins for whom everything was easy. Then they shouldered their packs and went between the drawn-back serpent head and the thrusting fist. When they looked again the wide view to the north was gone, closed off by granite walls slick with water. It was a place, Xantee felt, where a gool might find its way into the world after its journey along birthing veins deep underground.

The people would have told us, Lo said.

The people don't come here, they wouldn't know.

Let's get through it quick, Duro said.

But the way through was long and hard. They waded waist-deep through pools made by water oozing from crevices plugged with stringy moss, and emerged shivering, with no feeling in their legs. It was more ravine than pass. In places the walls leaned inwards, blotting out the sky. It was as though the body of the serpent and the arm attached to the fist rippled their stone muscles, keeping their contest alive. Yet there was no life – nothing in the pools, nothing in the hollows opening in the walls. The threat came from the cold and they forced themselves to jump and climb, and run where they could, to reach the end of the pass before nightfall.

The sun was hidden west of the mountains when they came out but sent shafts of light across the jungle confronting them. It lay in a wide basin rising at the far rim to another mountain range where snowfields shone pink and ice peaks gleamed. Rivers bent like knives, with flowering trees at their edges, coloured like rust.

Do we have to cross there? Lo whispered.

The Dog King's on the other side of those mountains, Xantee said.

Our grandfather, he said. I wish we could meet him halfway.

You can give up wishing. Let's get in those trees and make a fire, Duro said.

They slid and scrambled on scree slopes but soon found it too dark to keep on. There was nothing for it but to build a platform by scraping stones away and piling them up. They made a fire of branches hacked from mountain scrub, ate warmed strips of meat and drank water. Then they huddled close and slept as well as they could in the chill air.

Sun on their faces woke them. They stood and stretched and looked at the jungle they had to cross.

There's a gool in there somewhere, Lo said.

They strained their eyes, trying to see the cone of coldness the beast would make, but mist from swamps and slow-flowing waterways, and the sun's rays widening and diffusing, and the largeness, the lazy stretching out of the jungle, made the task impossible.

It'll take us weeks to get across, Duro said.

So, you want to turn back? Xantee said, letting her fear turn to anger at him.

I never said that. You need your breakfast. And I need a piss. Close your eyes.

The scree ran out in low hills, nodding together like heads. By midday the burning heat had Xantee longing for the cold of the pass. It was close to nightfall before they broke into flat land and saw the jungle in front of them – trees as solid-seeming as cliffs, with dark caves opening at the base.

Do we have to go in there? Lo said.

In the morning, Duro said.

No, I want to call the people tonight, Xantee said. She could not forget Hari wasting away.

They approached the trees, feeling their weight, feeling the greediness with which they fed on the earth. Behind a dark wall of growth they sensed the jungle teeming with life, all of it hungry, all of it intent on survival. Xantee wondered how many centuries – how many hundreds of centuries – the people with no name had spent reaching their state of perfect harmony with their surroundings. They had, in a way, conquered the jungle and, in another way, were part of it. She could imagine their dismay at the arrival of the gool, whose intention was, it seemed, to devour everything.

She and Lo spoke formally, in a soft clear voice: We are humans seeking your help, people with no name. We're searching for the place where the gool was born, to destroy it, and we ask your help to cross the jungle to the home of the Dog King, who knows the way.

Silence. No sound, no whisper from the trees. Only the humming, almost unheard, of a million insects, and the woofing and grumble of animals ending their day, and the crack, far off, of a rotten branch splitting from a trunk.

They're not here, Duro said.

They're here. We can feel them.

They like to play games, these Peeps. Why can't they just say yes or no?

Quiet, Duro, Xantee whispered. She had heard her name – and Lo his.

Xantee. Lo. And Duro, who can speak with us if he wishes. The way is open.

Duro, join with us, Xantee said.

He did so, clumsily, then with greater ease.

Xantee. Lo. Duro. We haven't spoken with humans before. But our brothers over the mountains told us you would come, and that you travel to fight the gool, which eats the world. Say what you would have us do.

Take us safely through the jungle. Show us where the Dog King lives.

The first we will do. But the Dog King is over the mountains, sometimes in the forest, sometimes on the plains, near the city that lies in pieces by the sea. We'll take you as far as we can.

Is there a gool on the way?

In the far mountains. We'll show you how to pass. Sleep now. In the morning follow.

How long to reach the mountains?

The sun will return as many times as you have fingers on your hands, then two more times.

Twelve days, Lo whispered.

Why can't they just say so? Duro said.

Xantee thought of Hari lying on his bed, growing thinner and weaker all the time.

Can we travel in the night? she asked.

You can travel and sleep when you need, the people said.

Then take us into the jungle now.

Xantee, Lo protested.

For Hari, she said.

We'll need torches, Duro said.

We can make light for you to see, the people said.

Then let's go now, Xantee said.

The sun made its sudden descent beyond the western mountains. The jungle, which had been blue and purple and grey, and rusty red with flowers, and yellow with slanting rays, turned black, as if to repel the travellers. As they approached a tiny seed of light appeared, floating ahead of them. It led the way, growing as it went into a pod, then into a globe enclosing them with light like a lantern of seed oil – except that it had no source and threw no shadows.

How do they –? Duro began.

They make it with their minds the way they make their song, Xantee said.

I can hear their song.

We'd be dead already without it, Lo said, pointing at a tree tiger lashing its tail on a branch ahead. As they approached it gave a howl of rage and leaped away into the cavernous dark.

They walked until midnight, safe in the double circle of light and song.

That's enough, Xantee, let's sleep, Lo said.

Let's eat first, Duro said.

They swallowed their meal, washed it down with water, laid out their mats, and slept until dawn lit the jungle enough for them to make out tree trunks gathered round like pillars and branches slanting down like a lean-to roof. Food again, then they went on, following the notes of the song like beads on a string.

Xantee counted the days: three gone, five, seven – and with

the hours gained by night-walking she worked out that seven made nine. So, three to go. Then they lost a day and night in a storm that attacked the jungle with great fists of wind and torrents of rain, and lightning that broke from its parent stem into a rain of bolts that brought trees crashing down. The people made them safe in a rock overhang, where they huddled behind a sheet of falling water – but each of them felt that this was a place where a gool might break out.

The next day they reached a river washing over its banks and running through the trees, so more time was lost.

Xantee gave up counting, but Duro, with his practical brain, worked the numbers out – time lost, time gained – until, as they settled down to sleep one night, he said, Two more days.

How do you know?

The Peeps told me.

They did not. They don't do sums.

All right. I'm keeping count. And maybe you haven't noticed but we're climbing. The creeks are running faster. Two more days.

Then where's the gool the Peeps said was here? It must be close, Lo said.

They'll tell us.

As if in answer, the people spoke for the first time in several days: A gool is on the mountain beyond the trees. A day, a night, a day, as Duro says, and you will see.

Is it big? Xantee whispered.

You will see.

They slept, then went on for two marches, with the land rising more sharply and the trees thinning out. Several times

70

Xantee thought she saw a flicker of people moving in the trunks, but she could never be sure – and she sensed that it was harder for them; they were nearing the edge of their domain.

A glimpse of mountain showed: an ice field shining, high. The jungle under-storey gave way to fern, then to sharp grass that cut their legs. They wrapped them in cloth from their packs and struggled on.

Xantee, Lo, Duro, this is the place where we must stop, the people said.

Is there – is there any way we can thank you for your help? Xantee said.

Kill the mother gool. She comes from the other side.

Of what? Duro said.

That lies beyond our knowing. But find where it is born, and learn what you must do.

Easy to say, Duro said.

Cross the mountains through the pass beyond the peak lifting like the bow of a sunken canoe. We cannot pass, but Dwellers who have come this way say it's hard but sure. On the other side the land lies easy to the jungle. Call for our brothers and sisters there.

Thank you.

What about the gool we have to pass? Duro said.

It lives below the peak. You must stay on the lower side of the gully. Unless it has grown the way lies open.

Will we see it?

See, and smell, and taste it in the air, and hear it mewing like a sick tree tiger. Don't go close. It lashes with its arms, and took a woman from a Dweller family passing through.

Xantee felt sick, remembering the gool that had dragged Sal and Mond towards its mouth and tangled Hari in its arms. This one would be bigger if it almost blocked the pass. And they would see it. It had no need to make itself invisible like the one Sal and Mond had found.

She thanked the people again but wasn't sure they heard. The suddenness of their going would offend her if she let it – but what they had done, keeping them safe, guiding them, went beyond friendship. They might never come close, never be seen or named, but Xantee felt her kinship with them.

Let's get out in the open. I want to breathe again, Duro said.

Don't forget to keep watch. We've got no help any more, Lo said.

They kept on through the dwindling trees into hills climbing to the face of the mountains. Looking back, they saw the jungle stretching north and east and west – the same jungle, Xantee realised, that Pearl and Hari had seen from another vantage point on their escape from the city. It had vanished into the distance, Pearl said, and seemed never to end. It still seemed never to end in the eastwards direction, and yet a great ocean lay beyond, the ocean that the Fish People, the Wideners, had sailed across to find a new home. She felt there was too much of everything – jungle, mountains, sea, too much space, too much past and future, too much time. She felt it crushing, not releasing, her and wanted to be home in the kitchen.

So do we all, Duro said.

Keep out of my head, she snapped.

The peak that jutted over the pass matched the people's description: the prow of a sunken canoe. The path to its base was strewn with boulders. Pools of water lay where it levelled out, but turned to grey mud as the travellers climbed.

It's made from dust, Duro said. See, it's everywhere. It must be what the gool shits out after it's eaten.

There's nothing for it to eat up here, Lo said.

It eats the rock. It eats anything. Smell it now? Taste it? Like fish bait ten days old.

I can feel the cold, Lo said.

I can hear it, Xantee said.

Stay here. Duro went forward and peered round a boulder, then recoiled. He looked again.

It's here. It's huge. I can't see how we can get past.

His face was white.

It's ten times bigger than the one that got Hari.

Lo and Xantee joined him.

The gool had been born from an oily crack in the mountainside. It bulged from darkness into the morning light, undulating beneath its skin. The main part of its body lay on the slope down from the crack, spreading, flattening, busy at its edges with a thousand tiny mouths eating whatever they found. Except for that ant-like busyness, and the organs turning under its skin, it was like a dead jellyfish on a beach – but larger, a thousand times larger than any jellyfish ever seen. The mewing Xantee heard was the sound of hunger coming from the mouths as they fastened on the living stone of the mountain slope. Every now and then a pit like a whale's blowhole opened in the gool's skin – there was no one place – and a puff of grey dust shot into the air.

Xantee, Duro, Lo could not speak. Each felt the same: there was no way they could fight this beast. There was no way it belonged in the world. Yet Xantee clung to one thing:

Barni found a way. Barni killed it, she whispered.

Barni was a story, Duro said.

Stories start in something real.

Maybe. What worries me is how we get past.

There's room, Lo said.

Remember it puts out arms like a grabfish, Duro said.

There's still room. We keep up hard against the opposite slope, where it widens out.

Can we climb those rocks? Xantee said.

If we have to.

Does it know we're here? Does it have eyes?

Does it have a brain? I can't feel one.

It's got hunger, that's its brain, Xantee said.

It's got eyes, Duro said. See those white things floating under its skin.

They look like a blind man's eyes, Xantee said.

They can see. They've seen us.

The thousand tiny mouths were still. The hungry undulations ceased their movement under the skin.

If we're going we go now, Duro said. Ready?

Ready, Lo said.

Yes, Xantee said.

They drew their black Dweller knives.

Duro led, going fast on the path while they were out of range, then veering a dozen of its body lengths away from the gool, climbing into the boulders on the side of the pass opposite the crack it had been born from.

The gool gave a loud mew – a dozen screeching cats. All its mouths had vanished and a maw the size of a brine tub opened in the part of its body nearest Duro. It grew six arms,

74

each coiled like a rope. They unrolled heavily, then fattened and leaped, and ran like hungry stoats across the path and through the boulders. Yet they thinned as they approached, as if the creature could not force enough of its bulk into the tubes it was shooting out.

'Come on,' Duro yelled. Come on: a silent cry, even louder. He scrambled a dozen steps clear of the probing arms. Xantee came behind him, also clear. She felt in greater danger from the stink and taste of the creature, and from its malevolence – it had a mind and hated them – than from its tentacles. Then, behind her, Lo gave a yell of fright. She turned and saw him overbalance, grab at the air – at nothing – then fall backwards from the boulder he had jumped to, and vanish into a crevice. She heard his cry of agony, and a long-drawn wail.

Lo!

She turned back, jumped, peered down, with Duro quickly at her side. Lo lay wedged between boulders that seemed to squeeze and crush him like closing hands. His face was turned up, agonised, his fingers clawed the rock.

My leg. My leg.

They climbed down to him, legs and arms braced on the slanting sides.

My leg. The gool.

They pulled him and slid him free, Lo screaming with pain. Below him, in the crack, a blind grey tentacle crawled upwards, seeming to sniff.

We can't lift him, Xantee yelled. He's too heavy.

Rope. In my pack, Duro said.

She scrabbled for it, pulled it out, uncoiled it, as Duro hauled Lo another metre.

75

Round him, under his arms. Tie it. Now take it up.

She climbed to the top of the boulder.

Lo, Duro said, we're going to pull you out. It's going to hurt.

But Lo had fainted. Xantee felt his consciousness blink out.

Duro swore. He drew his knife, slashed at the tentacle that had found his heel. Its stub fell away. He climbed the boulder crack to Xantee.

Right, pull. As hard as you can.

Painfully, slowly, they drew Lo to the surface and laid him on the smooth top of the boulder. Xantee freed the rope, which had bitten into his chest. Then she saw his leg. It was bent halfway down the shin, almost at right angles. A long gash in the calf welled blood. She thought she saw a gleam of bone.

Duro was busy scraping gool-slime from his heel.

Duro, his leg.

Yeah, broken. We've got to get him back to the Peeps. No, don't touch it. Let them.

Can they? Will they?

He'll die if they don't.

They stopped Lo's bleeding with a tightly bound cloth, then hoisted him, dragged him, back through the boulders away from the gool. Then they carried him, one on each side, down the path towards the jungle. Xantee dosed him with a pain-killing drug Tealeaf had given them, but still he wept and groaned with pain.

The western sky turned red. Darkness closed in. They were in the mountain scrub, not yet in the jungle. Xantee made a torch from twigs twisted round a shard of rock and they went on, with Duro carrying Lo on his back. She felt for animals with her mind, and sent out cries for the people. It was midnight before an answer came.

Stay where you are. Lay the hurt one down.

His leg is broken.

Lay him down. Then go.

I can't. He's my brother, Xantee cried.

Go. We'll take care of him.

His leg's smashed. He's bleeding.

We will take care. Go quickly or he'll die.

I can't –

Xantee, Duro said, trust them. They'll fix him. They said they would.

I want to see. I need to know.

You can't. You can't see them. And Xantee, they'll be letting him see them. No one else has, ever. So let them do it. Xantee, come.

They laid Lo down carefully. Xantee kissed him on the brow, on the lips. Her brother. She felt she was tearing her mind in half, leaving him – tearing her heart too.

Lo woke.

Xantee?

Lo, the people are going to look after you. They'll fix your leg.

Xantee, he whispered.

We've got to go.

He closed his eyes. Faintly, in a voice that drifted way, he said, Kill the gools. All of them.

We will.

She kissed him again.

The people were singing. With light and harmony they led Xantee and Duro up the track. Looking back, she saw another light dome settle on Lo, and thought for a moment she saw small figures moving in it.

We'll come back for you, Lo, she said, but felt no throb of consciousness in him.

An hour up the track the people left them. They made camp and ate and slept. In the morning they climbed to the pass. The gool was feeding on stone. Carefully they climbed and leaped past its tentacles. Without looking back – the beast seemed to suck in even a glance – they went on. The pass would take three days, the people had said. They ran when they could, trying to make up the time they had lost.

No one can come this way again. The gool's growing too fast, Xantee said.

Unless we kill the mother, Duro said.

She made no answer. This beast was only one of hundreds loose in the world. And she had lost her brother – abandoned him – Lo, who was part of her.

Tears streamed on her face as she ran behind Duro.

I hate you, gool. I hate you, she said.

SIX

Three days and nights of wet and cold. Painful scrambling followed by painful sleep. The view at the end of it was of a magic land: brown slopes, warm in the sun, forested hills falling away. Then a band of jungle, simmering with heat. Beyond that they could not see, but had a sense of plains and water. Clouds like puffballs drifted across the sky.

But look, Xantee said, pointing west. Coldness, like a flattened dome, uncoloured and painful to the eyes, floated on a pillow of grey mist. It was almost beyond the range of sight.

Another gool, Duro said.

It's the city. It's some sort of cloud hanging over Belong. I wish we had Hari. We need Hari.

No wishing. What we need is the Dog King. But first we have to rest.

He was right. She was exhausted. She had travelled too hard. She looked at her legs and arms – stained, bruised, stringy, scabbed; and she was the same inside, bruised in her mind.

Sleep for a while. For the afternoon. Otherwise you can't go on, Duro said.

Nor can you.

We've done the first part. Let's get ready for the second.

And after that the third.

Yes, the third.

He looked away at the cone of coldness and shivered.

They rested not one day but two, on a bank beside a stream flowing from an icy waterfall. They washed, then ate and slept, taking turns to listen for prowling animals. Xantee felt the pain of leaving Lo recede. She must trust the people. They would heal him. And he was free from the danger she and Duro must face. She watched Duro sleep through the second afternoon, turning her eyes from time to time over the forest. Somewhere in that huge land the Dog King had his camp. She had no idea what he would be like. All she could picture was a man with a furry body and the head of a dog, yet he was human like her. She expected him to be savage although, at times, like a father, she imagined he opened his arms to her. Pearl had told him Tarl could not 'speak', except with dogs, so she practised what to say: 'Tarl, I'm Xantee, Hari's daughter. Help us save Hari, Tarl.'

Duro stood up and stretched and she took her turn at sleeping. He shook her awake as the sun went down and gave her a meal of tubers he had found, baked in the embers of a fire. They broke the night into watches, then started south in the dawn, fresh and ready and fearful. The hills gave way to forested slopes, where trees with silver trunks and canopies of spoon-shaped leaves and tribes of shrieking, berry-eating birds reminded them of the forests by the Inland Sea. Their confidence returned. They did not need the people. The people were stupid to live in the jungle when they could live here.

But help Lo, look after Lo, Xantee whispered, contrite.

The next day they reached the edge of the plateau where the forest ended. The strip of jungle ran below like a wide, black river.

Climbing down took another day. They faced the close-packed, damp-leaved, indifferent trees – their third jungle. Neither wanted to go in. Perhaps alone, they would find their way through – eating berries and grubs, making paste from toadstools to ward off poisonous insects, making a wall with their minds to lock animals out; but there might be some new animal, too strong for them, or animals that hunted in packs – or, or . . . Xantee could not number the dangers. Snakes too quick for their defences, swamps that might suck them down, rivers too dangerous to cross – all the things the people had guided them past. They needed the people.

Call them, Duro said.

Join me. You've got to help.

They sent their voices out – their knitted voice. The answer came at once. The people had been waiting.

Tell us what you need.

Each word was like a breath of wind rounded at the edges.

Take us to the Dog King, who will guide us to the city to find the gool, Xantee and Duro said.

Follow us.

Wait, Xantee said. My brother, Lo. He's with your people on the other side of the mountains. He was hurt. Is he all right?

Our brothers and sisters told us you were coming. The word travelled far ways, through the narrow jungles at the mountains' end, by the sea coast, but no word of a human. Follow us.

Please –

Xantee, they don't know, Duro said.

They can find out.

They're not going to. Their minds don't work like ours. Trust them. Lo's all right. They said he would be.

She wanted to believe him, but she had heard Lo's pain, felt it inside her. She had seen white bone gleam in his leg. She needed a word – and would not get one.

Duro put his arm around her. 'Xantee,' he said, speaking aloud for intimacy. 'Leave him now. Leave him with the people. They'll cure him. Know it, Xantee. He's theirs and you're with me.'

After a while she said – but could not speak aloud: Yes, I know it.

Then come on. One more jungle. Let's just follow them.

The singing began as soon as they moved. The globe of light enclosed them when night fell. The people left food in their resting places. They found dry ground for them to sleep. A natural bridge made the way across one river. A dugout canoe waited at the next. Passing a swamp at the foot of a cliff, Xantee caught a faint smell of – not swamp water or mud, not something dead . . .

Gool, she said.

82

Yes, Duro said.

A gool we found before it grew, the people said. We wrapped it in our thoughts and it can't break out. When the mother dies it will die.

Are there any more?

Many, held in our traps. But those that have grown can't be stopped, they're too strong.

Are there any more big ones?

One by the sea coast. One in the pitted place in the western mountains. Others you have seen – two. But there are more in places we can't go.

How can we stop them? Xantee whispered.

The people did not answer.

Again Xantee and Duro went on – rivers, swamps, howling animals, shrieking birds. They slept and woke and had little idea of day and night.

We're turning west, Duro said.

Two more sleeps, two marches, the people answered. Then we reach the open forest, where we do not go. After that the dry plains and the city.

Where's the Dog King?

Somewhere, they said. You will find him.

One more river to cross, one more swamp to wade through. They burned off ticks that fastened on their legs – the people's singing had no effect on ticks. Then the land began to rise and the ground was firmer. There were fewer trees, with outcrops of grey rock here and there.

We must leave you, the people said.

How do we find him, the Dog King? Xantee said.

Travel in the silver trees, toward the setting sun. That is

83

where he rules. Listen for his dogs, but beware of them. Make yourselves safe where they can't go.

How –? she began, but the people were gone.

We'll never see them, she said.

They wouldn't be the people if we did, Duro said.

The rock outcrops grew more numerous, the jungle thinned. They broke through ferns and creeping vines into wide clearings where animals had dragged their prey. Gnawed bones and skulls lay here and there. Walking was easier but watching, listening, without the people, tired them. By nightfall the jungle lay behind and the silver trees, widely spaced, rustled their leaves in the evening air. They climbed a rock outcrop and found a warm basin near the top. They ate, then slept, taking turns to watch, Duro first.

In the morning Xantee said, Before we go I want to listen.

They're not here, they're in the jungle, Duro said.

I don't mean the people. Remember the voice you heard last summer. I've heard it too, only once, saying my name. I want to hear it again.

I think we should leave that voice alone.

Pearl hears it. Hari hears it. Pearl heard it first in a dream, then with Hari out in a boat. Now it speaks whenever they want. She told me just to wait.

Then wait.

Pearl and Hari hear it, Xantee said stubbornly.

Pearl and Hari are better people than us.

You needn't try, she said, but I'm going to.

She made herself ready, emptied her mind. Perhaps she should take her clothes off and be naked – but she put that thought aside, with Duro watching. Why though, should she care if he saw? He saw her swimming.

Angry, she turned away from him. Now her mind was cluttered and she must empty it again. Deliberately she set about it, and when it was done had no consciousness except a ghostly one of self – Xantee – but not a self able to get in the way.

She had first heard the wind and sea and forests and mountains breathe her name silently inside her diminished self one morning as she walked alone on the beach. It said nothing more, just Xantee, yet those two syllables united her with the thing that spoke – took everything from her, gave everything back, increased in all its cells by its oneness with the voice.

She had told no one, but Hari and Pearl knew, just as she had known when Duro heard. Don't go chasing after it, Pearl said. Wait and one day you'll hear it again. But you don't need to.

Xantee waited on the rock above the forest. I need you now, she thought – and that let in a part of herself, and nothing came, no whisper, no name. Tears ran on her cheeks, and soon she felt Duro's arm around her.

Go away, she said – but did not want him to. They sat until the sun warmed them through a gap in the trees. Xantee dried her face. I was stupid, she said.

Yes, you were.

I think we need the Dog King, not anything else.

We need more food. We need water.

I know.

You'll hear it again when you're not expecting to. It was like that with me. I think I fell over.

You would.

They climbed down from the rock. Water was easy to find; streams ran everywhere. Food was more difficult – berries that must be climbed for, fern roots that must be dug. They found enough, then went on through the trees. Soon they saw deer, too shy to be approached.

The dogs must hunt them, Duro said.

What dogs?

I've seen their scat, haven't you?

Old scat, fungus on it.

It means they hunt here.

They stood and listened but heard only the rustle of wind in the trees and the coughing of a stag far away.

The next day it was the same. They kept on towards the setting sun. There was no dog sign and only the sounds of trees and birds and deer.

I think the Dog King's just a story, like Barni, Duro said.

No. He's Hari's father, Xantee said.

Your gran'daddy.

Shh, Xantee said.

What?

Something touched me.

She meant in her mind: something that asked a question – Who? – and sniffed at her and gave the answer – Meat. She saw a flicker of black in the silver trunks.

Dog, she said.

Small one, Duro said. A scout. He'll go for the pack.

He had found dogs on his solitary trips over the mountains and knew how they hunted.

He'll bring them back and follow our scent. We can't get away.

We don't want to, Xantee said. I'm going to stop him. We'll send a message.

She glimpsed the dog again, running through the trees, and sent the command: Stop, dog. Come here.

She heard its yelp of surprise and felt its fear.

I won't hurt you. Come here.

Slowly it approached – a small, long-eared dog, heavy in its jowls. A dog, she supposed, skilled at following scent and finding prey. It fought against her command, writhing its hindquarters, snarling weakly. Xantee did not stop its advance until it was close enough to touch.

Dog, she said, lie down. Can you speak?

It made no reply, sent no image, but lay as she had told it and kept its teeth bare.

It can't speak, Duro said. Just tell it what to do.

Xantee was disappointed. If Tarl was able to talk with dogs she had supposed that dogs were able to reply. But perhaps he had a way of reading them. And this one, like all animals, must project images – of place, of food, of water, of prey. She had met with that in farm dogs and wild animals in the forest. Only the gool sent no images.

Dog, she said, tell me about Tarl.

The animal curled its lip back more.

Tell me about the Dog King.

It doesn't understand, Duro said. Let it go. It'll bring the others.

But will it bring Tarl?

We've got to take that chance.

Duro, if it doesn't they'll kill us. We can't hold off a whole pack. I'm going to let this one go, but hold him and follow him. He'll lead us to the others. We can feel if Tarl's there and if he's not we'll make this one forget and sneak away.

They'll scent us. You can't fool dogs.

Tell me a better way.

Duro shrugged.

So, Xantee said. She told the dog to stand, ordered it to stop snarling, reached out her hand and patted its head.

It hates me, she said. It's trying to bite me but it can't. All right, dog, take us to your pack. To the Dog King.

It turned from her and ran, but she slowed it to a walk and followed with Duro at her side.

They kept on till late in the afternoon, the dog in front as if unaware of the humans half a dozen steps behind. Then Duro said, I smell dogs. It's worse than a swamp.

I can hear them, Xantee said. They're in those rocks. Stop, dog.

The soft yelping, subdued barks, reminded her of children lined up at the village school. She patted the dog.

Now dog, you're free. Forget you ever saw me. And forget him – pointing at Duro. Have you forgotten? Good. Now go or you'll miss whatever it is they're feeding on.

The dog turned in a circle, as though chasing its tail, looked at them without seeing, then trotted away to the jumble of rocks where the pack was resting. It vanished as though through an open door.

Now, Xantee said, let's find out if Tarl's there.

They joined their minds and sent them after the dog, through the opening it had taken, and sensed, with disbelief, the size of the pack in the ring of stones – more than a hundred, more than two hundred. It was impossible to isolate one, except – they found the dog they had followed, but before they could fit themselves into his mind and see what he saw, they felt his blinding inrush of terror, heard him scream . . .

What? Duro said.

They're attacking him. They're killing him.

The screaming stopped but the hungry snarling and yelping went on.

You touched him, Duro said. He had your smell on him.

No, she wailed.

Let's get out of here. They'll follow his trail back.

I didn't mean him to be killed.

Come on, run.

They were too late. Dogs boiled out of the opening in the rocks, sighted them, poured at them, some silent, racing, others barking wildly.

Tree. Into a tree, Duro yelled.

They had time only to reach the nearest, a scaly trunked silver tree leaning at an angle. Xantee shinned up, with Duro half-running like a monkey behind. The leading dog, a giant hound, jumped at him and ran two steps on the trunk before sliding to the ground. Xantee climbed until she was in the branches. Duro found a place on the other side. They sat and panted.

The dogs were frenzied at the base of the tree, shrieking, running in circles. They were every size and colour, all filthy, with matted hair, all scabbed and scarred from fighting and hunting.

If they had any brains they'd bite the tree and bring it down, Duro said.

What will they do?

Wait until we starve and fall out.

Duro, we've got to call Tarl.

There is no Tarl.

One of them's in charge though. It's that big black one.

The dog was huge, the size of a tree tiger. It was smooth-haired, square-jawed, wide in its chest. Half its tail had been bitten off in a fight. Yet it had the best food and as much as it wanted, that was plain from the muscles that shifted under its skin. It looked up at Xantee and Duro with yellow eyes, seeing them as food and knowing it only had to wait.

It gave a short bark and the dog-clamour stopped. It barked again and most of the pack trotted off towards the rocks, leaving only a dozen at the tree. The pack leader circled, watching them. Then it gave a growl and turned away.

Talk to it, Xantee, Duro said.

She was still sickened by the death of the dog that had found them, but she cleared her mind, examined the leader until she was sure, then said, Dog.

It stopped in its tracks, turned slowly, looked at her, with hackles bristling on its spine.

Dog, she said, I'm Xantee. I want Tarl. I want the Dog King. Bring him to me.

It came back a few steps, as if to see her better. She got no picture from its mind. There seemed to be no image, even of herself. Yet there was a disturbance, like something stirring underwater. The dog was confused.

Dog, she whispered, go for him. Go for Tarl.

It's the name, she thought. It knows 'Tarl'.

The dog growled deep in its chest. Its skin shivered, like a horse getting rid of flies.

90

Tarl, she repeated. Bring Tarl.

It remained staring at her – hot yellow eyes with nothing in them but hunger for prey. But still, in its mind, a disturbance. Xantee felt she was in a contest of wills, and the dog, simpler than her, would win – except that she had Tarl. She pronounced his name, sent it into the animal, heavy and hard.

The dog shivered again. Then it gave a whimper, almost puppyish, and hung its head.

Tarl, Xantee said.

The dog met her eyes. An image came fleetingly – she had the impression of something human, man-shaped at least.

Bring him, she said. Bring Tarl.

The dog turned, walked to the rocks and vanished through the opening.

Now what? Duro said.

It knows him. So we wait.

There's only nine down there. We could put them to sleep one by one.

No.

We can't stay here all night. I'm getting a sore bum.

Eat something. Drink something.

They shared berries and water, and had barely finished when another dog walked from the rocks. It was smaller than the leader, as thick in its chest but shorter in its legs. It was yellow and black. After a moment it gave a woof.

A second dog, almost identical, joined it in the open, and with it came something that might be a man. He walked half bent, as though to be level with the dogs, but rose to his full height as he approached the tree.

He's not human, is he? Duro said.

Quiet, Xantee said.

Years of stooping had bent his back and lowered his head. Years of running with dogs had pulled his muscles askew and lengthened them so that they twisted like ropes across his limbs. His hair hung over his shoulders and down to his waist; grey hair, matted like a ram's fleece. He wore nothing: hairy shoulders, hairy loins. Nothing except a knife in a belt at his waist. It saved him from being a dog – and his eyes saved him. Xantee had half-expected hungry eyes, yellow eyes, but these, watching from beneath a fringe of knife-hacked hair, were the eyes of a man.

The dogs at the foot of the tree moved out of his way. The pair with him, yellow and black, stood at his sides. Like the pack leader they were well fed; but greedy, always hungry, Xantee saw, in the way of dogs.

The man said nothing, simply looked at Xantee and Duro. He touched his hands on his dogs and one of them yawned. The other seemed to grin. Tarl – he had to be Tarl – had said something to them. Fat ones, was that it? Or had Xantee misunderstood? He could speak with dogs, Hari and Pearl had said, but not with humans, unless with his tongue. Hari had told Xantee, though, that several times he had caught an unspoken whisper from Tarl.

She had to be quick. But before she could speak, Duro burst out: 'Say something, you. You're a man, not a dog.'

Tarl rolled his head as though avoiding a punch. His eyes opened wide. 'Ha!' he said.

Xantee knew she could go into his mind and control him, and that it was the safest way, but Pearl's and Hari's lesson was too strong: never invade someone's mind unless you do it to save your life. It hadn't come to that, not yet. Instead she said, 'How long since you've heard a human voice?'

'Ha!' Tarl said. He croaked and spat, then said, in a voice creaking with disuse, 'Words. Man words. All poison. All shit.' He loosened his knife.

'Try it,' Duro said. His own knife jumped into his hand.

'Boy,' Tarl said, his voice still creaking, 'my name is Knife. You think you can beat me. Climb down.'

'Stop,' Xantee cried. 'They're Dweller knives, not made for killing.'

'Dweller?' Tarl said, making the name as though his tongue was hinged.

'And your name isn't Knife or the Dog King, it's Tarl.'

'Tarl.' He closed his eyes, opened them, then dog-snarled with his lips, showing brown teeth, gapped and broken. 'Only dogs know that name. How do you know?'

Now, Xantee thought. She wet her lips. 'Hari told me. Your son.'

Tarl stepped back. The yellow dogs flanking him gave a yelp of dismay. Tarl shook his head, shaking something out – anger? pain? – and his knife, quicker than Duro's, jumped into his hand. Xantee's mind was faster. Now was a time to save her life.

Stop, she said. And said to Duro, who had raised his arm to throw: Stop, Duro. I've got him. Put your knife away.

Tarl's eyes were burning. She was holding him only lightly – enough to stay his knife-hand.

Tarl, listen to me. I don't want to be in your mind. I'll speak to you in a voice you can hear when you put your knife away. But I'm going to tell you about Hari.

93

He shook himself, bent and groaned, trying to break free. The nine dogs about the tree slunk away to the rocks, and the yellow pair whimpered.

Tarl, put it away, she said. Then we'll talk.

He was strong. His will seemed as strong as the gool's, but she held him, and at last he slid the knife into its sheath.

Now, Tarl, I'm going to let you go. Then we can talk.

She released him, and he staggered and put his hands on the dog's backs to feel their warmth. Then he looked at Xantee.

'That's a Dweller trick, getting in my head.'

'I'm sorry. Can we come down?'

'Tell the boy to keep his knife in his belt.'

'Yes.'

'Or I'll kill him.'

'He won't touch it.'

Unless I have to, Duro told her.

I'll do the talking, Duro. You keep quiet and keep still.

They climbed out of the tree. Tarl could have killed her then with no trouble, but he stood and watched with, Xantee thought, his hackles raised, like his yellow dogs. He worked his lips and seemed to sniff her odour.

'Talking hurts my mouth.' He studied her, narrow-eyed. 'You're Company.'

'No. Company's gone. Company's dead.'

'Not white, not black. Half Company. Blue eyes.'

'I get them from my mother.'

'And the boy,' Tarl said. 'He's Company. Soon I'll kill him for that.'

'My father died fighting Company and the clerks,' Duro said.

'No matter, boy. White skin dies.'

'No one dies,' Xantee said. 'And some are alive you think are dead. My mother, Pearl.'

'Pearl?' Tarl said, stepping back from her.

'She gave me my blue eyes. And my father gave me my skin. Not black, I'm sorry. Brown. His name is Hari.'

'No,' Tarl said. 'Hari's dead.'

'He's alive. And Pearl is alive.'

'He jumped from the cliff. He chose her.'

'He chose her because they were going to kill her.'

'She was Company.'

'No, she was Pearl.'

'And he died. I saw.'

'You saw what Hari wanted you to see. And wanted Keech to see, and all the burrows men. And the women too, from Bawdhouse.'

'No.'

'Yes, Tarl. Listen. Hari's your son. You taught him. His mother died in the sickness and he rode on your back in Blood Burrow until he could run by himself. You taught him how to use a knife and how to kill king rats. You showed him where to hide when the Whips came hunting. But the Whips caught you and took you to People's Square. Hari told me and my brother, Lo.'

'Lo?'

'Yes, named after the Survivor, Lo, who taught Hari to speak with dogs and rats, and with him too, without using his tongue.'

'No.'

'Listen, Tarl. In People's Square you tried to kill the clerk –'

'My knife was slippery with blood. It slipped in my hand.'

'Then Hari cut you free, but the Whips caught you again. Hari escaped. He swam in the swamp and climbed through a hole in the wall, and he promised to save you from the place they were taking you to. Shall I name it, Tarl?'

'No. No,' Tarl whispered, sinking to the level of his dogs as though strength had drained from his legs.

Xantee whispered it. 'They took you to Deep Salt.'

A wailing sound came from Tarl's mouth – grief, terror, agony of mind. He fell to his knees and put an arm round each of his dogs. They licked him, trying to comfort him.

'And there, Tarl, you saw the grey ghosts –'

'No. No more.'

It's enough, Xantee. Don't hurt him, Duro said.

But Xantee had one more thing to say: 'Hari saved you. Hari kept his promise. He came and saved you.'

Tarl stayed kneeling. Tears ran from his eyes on to the dogs' snouts. Xantee waited. She kept herself from looking in his mind. At last he stood up and wiped his face.

'Girl,' he said, 'others were there. Anyone could have told you. Not Hari. Hari died.'

'No, he lived.'

'He chose the white bitch and jumped off the cliff with her. They smashed to pieces on the rocks.'

'Tarl, listen again. Hari was your son. You taught him to think; you taught him how to save himself. Do you think when he explored the Company mansions, watching through the windows as servants carried food to the tables and the fat Company bosses ate with grease on their chins, and their pretty women put it in their mouths with silver forks – did he tell you all that, Tarl? Yes, he told you. But do you think as he watched he had no way of escape if the guards saw him? He knew the cliffs. He knew the one place he could jump, if the tide was high and the wind was blowing big waves in. The wind was blowing that night, Tarl, the tide was high, when Burrows signed a treaty with the Clerks, and you threw the Company princeling off the cliff and your dogs killed Ottmar. Keech found Pearl. He showed his followers her hair, he showed her eyes. And Hari saved her –'

'Others could have told you this,' Tarl cried.

'Look at me, Tarl. Do you remember Pearl? Am I like Pearl?'

'No.'

'Am I like Hari?'

'No.'

He would not look at her.

He's not going to believe you, Xantee, Duro said.

She had one more thing to try.

'Tarl,' she said. He looked at her. 'Your name is Tarl. And Tarl the Hunter. And Knife. And the Dog King. Many names. But you have one more. The clerk burned it with acid on your forehead in People's Square. No one sees it. You hide it with your hair. No one knows that name any more. But Hari knew it and Hari told me. Shall I tell you your other name, Tarl?'

His hand had risen – he could not stop it – and clamped on his forehead. Under his black weather-beaten skin he was sickly white.

'You can't hide it from me, Tarl,' Xantee said. 'Your other name is DS936A.'

His mouth widened in agony. His voice was like a frog's croak. 'No one . . .'

'Except me and my brother Lo and Hari and Pearl.'

'DS,' Tarl said, 'is . . .'

'Yes, I know,' Xantee said gently. 'DS is Deep Salt. The number is your number. And A is your grading. The clerk had never given an A before.'

Tarl rose to his feet, a movement so quick Xantee had no time for thought. He ripped his knife from his belt and threw. She thought it was meant for her, but it split the gap between her and Duro and thudded into the tree ten metres away. And as quickly as Tarl had moved Duro moved: changed his lunge at Tarl, turned and made an underhand throw, and his knife whacked into the tree a finger's width from Tarl's.

Xantee held the dogs still.

Tarl panted. Then he changed to deep breaths, calming down. At last he said, 'Yes, that's my other name.'

'I'm sorry,' Xantee said. 'Can I let the dogs go?'

She heard him say something to them – a tongue she did not know – and she released them. They sank at Tarl's feet and watched him, waiting to be told what to do.

He turned to Xantee. 'Yes,' he said, 'you look like him. My son, Hari. And the Company whore he chose ahead of me. And you, boy –' he looked at Duro – 'you learned that throw from Hari.'

'Yes,' Duro said.

Tarl nodded. 'So Hari lives.'

SEVEN

'No,' Xantee said, 'Hari dies.'

Just tell him straight, Duro said. You've played enough games.

He walked to the tree, pulled out the knives, slid his in its sheath, and after holding the black knife a moment, admiring its balance and blade, handed it to Tarl.

'Hari said you were the best knife-thrower who ever lived.'

Tarl took the knife but ignored him. 'Dies?' he said in a stunned voice.

'She means, he's dying if we don't save him,' Duro said. 'He fought with a gool. He saved two of our people. But the gool wrapped an arm round his neck. We've stopped it feeding on him but we can't make it let go.'

'Gool?' Tarl said.

'It comes out of the rocks, out of the wet. It eats everything.'

'I've seen one.'

'What do the dogs call it?'

'Dogs don't give names. They know by smell. I call it Thing. It lives by the black river that runs out of the jungle. It's as big as the swamp in People's Square. It took four of my dogs. Do you say there are others?'

'Everywhere. Eating everything.'

'And Hari fought it?'

'It was a small one, as small as a bear. He cut off two of its arms but one tied itself around his neck. We can't get it off.'

'What do you want me to do?'

'Tarl,' Xantee said. She saw he preferred talking with men – Pearl had warned her. 'We'll tell you when we get away from here. But we need you to come with us.'

'To help Hari?' Tarl said.

'To kill the gool and save Hari's life.'

'No one can kill it. Thing. Gool.'

'There's a way if we can find it. You can help us. But we need to get out of here, away from your dogs.' She meant the pack in the rocks.

'Can you stop them from attacking us?' Duro said.

'Until they get hungry.'

'Will you come?'

'For Hari?'

'Yes, for Hari.'

Tarl knelt suddenly and drew the two black and yellow dogs close to his sides. He had a way of 'speaking' Xantee could not follow – quick and easy. Smell was in it, hunger too, and fear, bravado, loyalty – dog things.

In a moment he stood up. 'We'll come.'

'Now?'

'Now. Where to?'

'To the city. The burrows. To Blood Burrow.'

Tarl blinked. 'Why there?'

'Can we go? It's getting dark. We've got to find a place to eat and sleep. You lead. We'll follow.'

She saw, in a moment, that he was used to leading, although the two dogs scouted at the sides. He went fast through the darkening trees, finding his way as easily as if he were on a road. Now and then they heard a reassuring bark from one of the dogs.

After several hours he stopped suddenly. She heard him call the dogs in.

'Eat,' he said to Xantee and Duro.

'Here?'

'Here.'

'What about you?'

'In the morning.'

The dogs trotted in, one from the left, one from the right.

'What are their names?'

'They don't have names.'

It was easy enough to tell them apart – one was a dog, the other a bitch. So, Him and Her, she told Duro.

How about Talk and Do?

Shut up, Duro. Do you trust him?

Yes.

I do and I don't. He's like a dog. He is a dog. He could turn savage.

He won't. He wants to help Hari.

Tarl lay down with a dog on either side. They seemed, all three, to sleep instantly. Xantee and Duro ate – grubs and berries, the last of their food. They drank water from their flasks, leaving enough for the morning. Then they unrolled their mats and wrapped themselves in their blankets. One of the dogs was snoring. The other, Xantee realised, had opened its eyes and was watching them. It was Her. Tarl had woken too. She saw his eyes gleam in a shaft of moonlight angling through the trees.

'Now,' he said, 'tell me why Blood Burrow.'

'Can't it wait till morning? We're tired.'

'Tell it now.'

'Shouldn't someone be watching? There might be animals hunting.'

'Nothing hunts.' All the same he spoke with Her and she stood up and stretched and walked into the trees.

'Now.'

Xantee told it, all of it: Hari's fight with the gool, then his wasting away; Tealeaf's tale of Barni and the stars (she told it carefully, not sure Tarl would understand); Tealeaf's recollection of Dweller tales about Belong, with its galleries and libraries; and then their journey and Lo's accident and leaving him with the people with no name.

'We've crossed two mountain ranges and walked through three jungles to reach you, Tarl.'

'Why me?'

'Because you can take us to the burrows. You can help us find the books that will tell us what Barni's story means.'

'What are books?'

'Can you read, Tarl? Nor could Hari. Pearl taught him. She taught me. Books are stories made with marks that turn into words you can say. They're made from goatskins, the marks on them are made with – with soot, with dye, with whatever makes a mark and stays in place. Sometimes the skins are rolled on sticks. Sometimes the makers cut them in squares and sew them together. Tarl, did you see them in the burrows? There were huge rooms full of them.'

'If books are made from goatskins the rats have eaten them.'

'But if the rooms are locked . . . ?'

'Not in Blood Burrow. The rooms were broken open long ago. All rooms.'

'The other burrows then?'

'Keech and Keg? I was Blood. I was dead if I went there. These books you talk about might have been in the city Company built. I never went in the city either.'

Xantee shook her head. 'Company had no books except their tallies of what they bought and sold. But in Belong there was everything, before Company came.'

'Take us there, Tarl, so we can look,' Duro said.

'Keech is in the burrows. And the Clerk is in the city, behind the walls. They fight each other. They hate each other. But they hate me more. It's death for me to go there.' He smiled – more a baring of his teeth than in amusement. 'But what is death except to die? I'll take you to Blood Burrow, and to Keech and Keg and Bawdhouse and Port if I have to. And into the Clerk's city. For Hari.' He looked at Xantee. 'And for you. You have my blood.'

'Thank you, Tarl,' Xantee said.

'But you must keep quiet and not talk. Women don't talk.'

She heard Duro laughing inside, but stopped herself from bursting out at him. She would talk all she wanted in her head. She was moved too, suddenly, by Tarl's acceptance that they shared blood.

Duro said, 'Why do Keech and the Clerk hate you?'

'The Clerk blames me for his crippled arm. Did Hari tell you? When he tried to cut me free in People's Square he made the horses bolt and the Clerk's cart tipped over. His arm was crushed on the stones. Now it hangs at his side like a rotten branch. And all the time it hurts him. It stabs. Sometimes he howls in the night. That is good. I think of it as I lie down to sleep. But he blames me. He sends men out to capture me and I lead them into swamps, where they drown. They're food for the dogs.'

Duro swallowed. It was more than he wanted.

'What about Keech?'

'He has always hated Blood Burrow and I'm Blood Burrow.' He seemed to think that was enough.

'What happened on the hill, Tarl, after Pearl and Hari jumped?' Xantee said.

Tarl looked at her briefly. 'Blood Burrow and Keech Burrow fought. We killed each other while the Clerk laughed inside himself. Keech had more men but I had my dogs. The other burrows joined with Keech and drove us from the hill. We ran for Blood Burrow. And then Blood Burrow turned on me; they blamed me. So I ran again, with my dogs, and came to the forest, where I live a better life than back there.' He put a hand on the dog at his side and it wagged its tail.

'What happened back there?'

'Keech made himself king of the burrows. There's no Blood Burrow any more. No Keg, no Bawdhouse, it's all Keech. But he hates me, just like the Clerk. He blames me for losing the city and the heights and for the clerks breaking the treaty we made that night. So he sends men out to hunt me. I deal with them in the same way.'

'And you're the Dog King?' Duro said.

'Men call me that. But there's no king. There's only the leader of the pack. Once it was Dog. Did Hari tell you about Dog?'

'Yes,' Xantee said.

'He was leader. I was – they did not know what I was. They let me live because of Dog and because I taught them new ways of hunting and killed game out of their reach.' He touched his knife. 'Then Dog grew old and they killed him.' He saw Xantee start. 'A younger dog challenged him. Dog lost and the pack tore him apart. It's the way. They let me live. I was still useful. And what I tell them to do they do. But the black dog is the leader. And when I'm too old to run with them –' he shrugged – 'they'll kill me too.'

'Can't you get away?'

'Why? The pack's my home. I'll live with them and die their way.'

'We can take you to Hari.'

'No. He chose another way.'

'But you'll help him?'

'He's my son.' But he laid his hand on the dog at his side – his son too?

'Is that one, and the other one, do they come down from Dog?' Duro said.

'They have Dog's blood. Now –' he turned from them

– 'you've told me. The city's west. The burrows are west. Tomorrow we'll start. Sleep now.'

He lay down and closed his eyes.

Xantee and Duro stretched out on their mats and pulled their blankets tight. Soon, although there were many new things to think about, they slept too.

EIGHT

Xantee did not count the days; she thought of Hari dying. The forest ran on, never changing, until Duro showed her that the trees were thinning out and getting smaller. They shrank to head height, dry and twisted, then gave way to scrub with knife-point leaves and hidden thorns. Another day in the scrub, with the land falling away in a slope too gradual to notice. After that, bare hills where the sun beat down and fangcats hunted. The dogs would have fought them, and Tarl too, with his knife, but Xantee and Duro pushed the creatures away with their minds. Tarl shook his head contemptuously.

'Dweller tricks,' he said.

They were two days in the hills. One of the dogs ran ahead, scouting from side to side. The other stayed in reach of Tarl's hand. In the mornings, when Xantee and Duro woke, all three were gone, and they came back bloodstained, the dogs red on their muzzles and Tarl on his beard. He threw a lump of meat to Xantee and Duro and they cut it thin and charred it on a low fire. Tarl refused meat that was cooked. He seemed more savage, he talked less, but was always in conversation with the dogs. Yet Xantee was surer of him, less afraid that he would turn on them. Hari was her father and Tarl was Hari's father. It was enough. She wished only that he would tie a cloth about his loins, but decided it was better not to offer him one.

They walked down a twisting gully to the edge of a steep incline. Thunder clouds like bread dough swelled in the south, while westwards veils of rain dropped across the sky. Then a burst of sunshine lit a patch of white that gleamed like pearl shell.

The sea, Xantee said.

'The sea,' she said to Tarl.

He showed no interest, but called a halt. They rested with their backs against a wall of warm rock. Yellow plains stretched away almost to the edge of the distant rain. At the margin Xantee saw a grey uneven line running inland from the sea.

Duro, that's the city.

No.

Yes. 'Tarl, is that the city?'

'City,' he grunted, and sucked at the gnawed bone he had carried all morning. He broke it at the joint and threw half to each of the dogs.

Belong, Duro whispered. I was born there.

They watched almost without breathing, although nothing moved except the thunderheads. The city was only a thin grey line. In a moment the rain slid down and hid it. Yet, Xantee thought, it's more – more than just a line. She had sensed – or had she seen? – a film of something lying over it, like the film of lost life on the eye of a netted fish lying in the bottom of a dinghy. She shivered. There was a gool in there, perhaps the mother gool, the largest one. What better place could it have for its home?

She tried to eat but found she could not swallow.

Pearl and Hari must have come this way, Duro said.

Yes, Xantee said, although she thought it had been further west. Pearl and Tealeaf, escaping from the city, and Hari searching for his father. They had crossed the plain into these hills. The river down there, pink in the sun, must be the river where Hari had killed Pearl's brother, Hubert. He had named one of the twins after Hubert – making up for the life he had taken – while Pearl had named the girl twin Blossom after her sister thrown from the cliff.

Xantee shivered. So much killing. And it seemed there might be more to come.

'Where are the burrows, Tarl?'

'On the other side of the city.'

'And that's where Keech is? And the Clerk is in the city?'

'Let the boy ask.'

'What happened to the workers, Tarl?' Duro said. 'They had an army. My father was in it till he died.'

'Some joined the clerks. Others ran away into the plains and made towns. Maybe they're still there, I don't know.'

He said something to the dogs and Him stood up and stretched and trotted away.

'Where's he going?'

'To find a cave. The storm is coming.'

109

It lasted the rest of that day and all the night. They stayed in the cave the dog had found. At dawn the rain and thunder rolled away. The plain was washed clean and the distant city had turned black.

'Can we get there today?' Xantee said.

'Look at the river,' Duro said.

It foamed and twisted and from high on the cliff they heard stones rumbling in its bed.

Tarl did not seem worried. He led them down a goat track to the plain. They waited beside the river and by nightfall it was low enough to cross. Tarl carried a dog under each arm. The water was still strong enough to sweep them away.

They pushed on through the night, making up time, and hid in scrub below the city wall as the sun came up.

'Give me a piece of your blanket, girl,' Tarl said.

He tore a strip from the side and tied it about his waist and between his legs.

So I get cold at night, Xantee thought. Why can't Duro get cold?

I'm bigger than you, he replied, hearing. My blanket hardly covers me.

'Tarl,' he said, 'are we going into the city first or the burrows?'

'Burrows,' Tarl said.

'I can't go there. I'm white.'

'White, brown, black, doesn't matter. Men go where they go. They fight for whoever feeds them best.'

They had reached the city close to the end of the northern wall. It turned sharply south and there it had been broken to half its height by cannon bolts in one of the forgotten wars.

Duro clambered among the fallen stones, climbed the wall like stairs and looked over the city.

Xantee went up beside him. The neighbourhood below them had seen heavy fighting and scarcely any building was whole. They had been mean buildings to start with, hovels for the class of workers little better than slaves. Now they were broken, bent, tipped over, rusty, rotten. They were weed-infested, and puddled in their yards and streets from the night's rain. She saw rats running here and there. The wars had been a victory for rats. She saw no people, or signs of them.

Tarl climbed up beside them.

'The burrows are worse,' he said.

The fighting had been less fierce further into the city. Houses stood undamaged, sturdier than the ones by the eastern wall, worker dwellings in wood and stone. Even there no people moved.

'That's where I was born,' Duro said. 'My father worked for Ottmar in his salt warehouse.'

Tarl gave a growl at the words 'Ottmar' and 'salt'. At the foot of the wall the dogs heard him and whimpered.

The sun came out from behind clouds and lit the hill where the Family mansions had stood. It picked out buildings in the city centre, some four or five storeys high. Their marble walls and columns turned pink – but they too were pocked with holes as black as bat caves. It was, Xantee supposed, the part of the city called Ceebeedee, where Company's business had been done. Smoke rose here and there from morning fires, and she supposed people lived in the empty offices. She had thought the Clerk would live on the hill, in

111

the great Ottmar mansion, but straining her eyes, she saw no sign of life. She made out only shapes that might be trees and broken walls.

'Down,' Tarl said suddenly. He pulled them on to a lower part of the wall as something whined over their heads.

'Robber. Slingshot,' he said.

'Will he follow us?'

'The dogs will have him if he does.'

They kept on southwards through the scrub, staying clear of the city wall. It turned west, dropping down a long slope to the sea, and there before them, stretching mile on mile, lay the burrows. Xantee would not have believed so much desolation possible. Near at hand shattered stone and brick and twisted iron and rusty pipe were locked in a sinewy growth of creeping scrub. Once it was the outer edge of a great city. This rubble had been houses, shops, schools, taverns before the great Company ship, Open Hand, sailed into the harbour. She looked across the ruins, trying to identify Port, where the ship had berthed, but saw only broken walls, spiked and stepped and slanting, against the white sheen of the sea.

'Where's Blood Burrow?' she whispered.

'No Blood Burrow any more,' Tarl said.

'Where was it?'

'By the wall. You went west to Keg and south to Keech. Everything is Keech now. Keech is king of the burrows.'

'Where is he?'

'See where the smoke comes up. That will be his fires.' He pointed at a brown smudge south, towards the sea. 'But he moves. Keech doesn't leave his people alone. He knows the danger. He rewards. He punishes. No one knows if Keech will be behind him when he turns around.'

'Can we keep away from him?' Duro said.

'We can try. But I only know Blood Burrow and he's got men everywhere.'

'Xantee and I can find them. We can make them forget.'

'You'll need to.'

'Are we going in now?' Xantee said. She felt it would be like walking into a swamp, like the jungle, but without the Peeps to keep them safe.

'That's what you wanted, girl,' Tarl said.

'What will we do for food and water?'

'The rain's coming again. No shortage of water. No shortage of food either –' he smiled his snarling smile – 'if you can eat what I kill.'

He meant rats. She saw he was hungry for rats. She remembered that Hari had eaten them, had grown up on rats, and Pearl had eaten rat too, when she was ill and he was nursing her. If her mother could, her mother raised on spiced lamb and sugar and confections . . .

'We'll eat what we have to,' Duro said.

'Yes,' Xantee said.

Tarl nodded. He led them into the burrows, with the dog, Him, scouting and the bitch at his side.

Duro took Xantee's hand to give her courage. She felt him take courage from her.

NINE

The first day they travelled safely, with the dogs alert and Xantee and Duro probing with their minds. Several times they led Tarl away from the course he wanted to take – runways, mazes in the rubble – away from bands of Keech men, patrolling randomly. Surprise was a tactic Keech had perfected. Twice they came across bodies of scavengers or defectors, punished in the places they were caught.

Too much killing, Xantee thought. Rain fell on the burrows, then the sun beat down from a hard sky, making flat surfaces steam and the ruins hiss like an oven, but she felt cold everywhere – the coldness of humans without pity and the unnatural coldness of the gool.

Tarl had made them cut branches of scrub. When night fell they found a den where no light escaped and made a fire. They scorched the meat he brought and ate it half raw.

For Hari, Xantee thought, swallowing.

'Where are we going?' she asked.

'We're nearly through Blood Burrow. Tomorrow it's Keg.'
Tarl grimaced. Those names were lost. 'If these books you
want are anywhere they're south of Port. There was a park
by the sea. Hari went there. He went everywhere. Buildings
called Music Hall and Art Hall.' Tarl shook his head. He had
no idea what art and music were. 'If there were books . . .'

'Book Hall?' Xantee said.

'Hari never said that name. He said the park had stone
arms and legs, and heads of horses, and a fangcat killing a
sheep.'

'Statues,' Xantee said. 'Like Cowl the Liberator in People's
Square.' Hari had told her about Cowl.

'Cowl Bigmouth,' Tarl said. 'The bolt cannons broke the
ones in the park to pieces.'

And the rats have eaten the books, Xantee thought. But they
had to find out. She could not think of anything else to do.

They set out again in the morning. In the part of the
burrows that had been Keg, women and children had built
shelters in the ruins. As Tarl had said, they were every colour,
some even had the reddish-brown of the south, like Sal and
Mond. There was no way round them. Children approached,
begging, but the sight of the dogs sent them scuttling away.
There were no dogs in the burrows any more. Keech had
wiped out all that had not fled with Tarl.

'These people will tell the patrols we're here,' Tarl said.

'We can make them forget,' Duro said.

'There are too many. Capture one of the scouts. Make him
tell us where Keech is.'

They found a hiding place behind a wall half fallen into a
hallway. Tarl and the dogs slept – they could sleep at will –

while Xantee and Duro kept watch. Women passed, carrying buckets of water from a well at the end of the street, but it was midday before a man appeared. He had the quick movements of a scout, and a way of shrinking into doorways and emerging like a shadow. He stopped suddenly outside the place where the travellers were hidden.

Duro, he's seen the dogs' footprints.

Grab him, Duro said.

They acted together – the simple command Pearl and Hari had taught them: Be still.

The man – a ragged man, white-skinned but blotched with some disease – straightened, grew rigid, turned as though a magnet drew him.

Stand still. Lean on the wall. You're having a rest.

Tarl and the dogs had woken. The dogs were growling.

'Keep them quiet, Tarl,' Duro whispered. 'What do you want us to ask this man?'

'If Keech knows I'm here.'

Xantee spoke: What's your name?

'Hans,' whispered the man.

Tarl shifted angrily. 'Speak out loud so I can hear.'

'Does Keech know Tarl has come?'

'He knows there's a man with dogs. A man with dogs is Tarl.'

'What's he doing?'

'He's sent out scouts. He's sent patrols.'

'Where do you report to him?'

'In People's Square. He'll be there with his fighting men tonight.'

'Ask him why People's Square,' Tarl said.

Xantee asked, although Tarl could have put the question himself.

'Keech says Tarl will go to Blood Burrow,' Hans said.

Tarl smiled and nodded. 'Now ask him where the Clerk is.'

'Hans, where's the Clerk?'

The man gave a start, as though of pain, and Xantee, who was holding him only lightly, and without Duro's help, nearly lost him. She took a firmer hold.

'Where's the Clerk, Hans?'

'His name must not be spoken,' Hans whispered. He writhed against the wall.

'Why?'

'Keech has forbidden it. Any man who speaks his name dies.'

'Why?'

'Hatred,' Hans whispered.

'Hatred for the Clerk?'

'Yes. Hatred for . . .' He could not say the name.

'Where is he, Hans? The man whose name you can't say?'

'In the city. In Ceebeedee.'

Tarl grunted. 'Enough. Bring this Hans in here so I can kill him.'

'No. No killing. Duro and I will make him forget.'

'If you can.'

'We can.' Duro?

They spoke together, silently: Hans, you've talked to no one. You've seen no sign of dogs. Go, and keep forgetting.

The man woke from his trance. He turned in a circle, as though finding out where he was. He scrubbed out the dog marks with his foot then slunk away.

117

'Now,' Tarl said, 'we go to People's Square.'

'No, you said Port.'

'I want to have a look at Keech. I know places to hide.'

'But Hari's dying.'

'One more day. Then Port.'

There was no shifting him. But every step they took back the way they had come seemed like a weakened heartbeat – seemed like Hari fading away. They hid from scouts and patrols. In the afternoon Tarl veered from their previous course, turning into alleyways crushed by walls that had collapsed. They crawled through openings barely wide enough for a man, grazing their skins, sinking their hands in slush and water. They climbed into rooms with fallen ceilings, where fires had been lit in corners and soot had painted flame shapes on the walls. The bones of ancient feasts littered the floors.

'Where?' Xantee panted.

'Soon,' Tarl said.

The rooms grew bigger. Richer houses, she supposed, from the days before Company had destroyed Belong. Giant beams, hacked and knife-shaved for kindling wood, climbed like branches into floors above. They went up, Tarl and Duro carrying the dogs, and came into a hall with the ceiling unbroken and star-shaped holes in the walls.

'Hari came here,' Tarl said.

It had been a place for feasting and dancing, and Xantee remembered Hari speaking of a room with pictures on the floor made from pieces of coloured stone. This was the room: horsemen in green cloaks hunting deer, women stepping out of baths filled with blue water, a yellow sun, a red fire in a kitchen with a pig roasting on a spit . . . Some of the pieces had been dug out with knives but enough were left for Xantee to see how skilled the makers had been. If they could do this they could make books and explain the story of Barni and the stars.

'Come,' Tarl said impatiently.

'Hari told us about these pictures. Duro, see, women dancing. And here are men playing instruments. Here's one with a flute like Pearl's.'

Duro cleared stones and dust with his foot. 'And here's a man unrolling a book,' he said.

'Where? *Yes.* And see behind him, lots of books stacked on the walls. Tarl, do you know where this place was?'

'No place,' Tarl said. 'Company burned and broke everything. Now follow me, and quiet. People's Square is on the other side of the wall.'

That silenced her. People's Square, where the Clerk had branded Tarl and Hari had escaped the Whips by swimming deep in the swampy pool surrounding the statue of Cowl the Liberator. He had climbed into this room and seen these pictures . . . He seemed to be standing at her side, she felt the warmth of his arm . . .

Come on, Xantee, Duro said.

Hari, we'll save you, she thought, and although it was too far she sent the message anyway, from this room, across Blood Burrow, over the forests and jungles and mountains, over the Inland Sea, to the room where he lay. Perhaps he would hear a whisper that would help him draw another breath.

Tarl had started off. The bitch, Her, nudged Xantee with its nose. She followed. Tarl led them through another big room, then smaller ones, some filled with rubble almost to the place where the ceiling had been.

'Quiet,' he whispered.

As they passed a jagged hole in the floor they saw a cobbled street below and Xantee knew this was one of the gates leading into the square. It allowed her to get her direction fixed. They had reached the western edge. She smelled swamp air rising through the hole.

Soon Tarl turned again, into ruins on the southern side of the square. He stilled Xantee and Duro with his hand and sent one of the dogs ahead, trusting its nose ahead of Xantee's probing. She could have told him no one was there, and that there were people in the square.

Duro, how many?

Hard to tell. Fifty. Sixty.

Tarl beckoned them. They went ahead, crawling in narrow spaces, then found more height and walked upright. Xantee sensed that Tarl had not been here before but knew it all the same, from outside in the square. It must be where Hari had lain and watched men tie his father to a cart and lead him away to Deep Salt.

The dog stopped in a small room with a boarded-up window. People had lived here since Hari's day then abandoned it. Again there were bones on the floor. The burrows were a bone yard, Xantee thought. One of the boards had fallen at an angle, giving a view of the square. Tarl held Duro back. He looked out, while the dogs put their noses to a crack lower down, sniffing the unwashed human smell rising from the square.

'Keech men,' Tarl whispered; then, with a quiver almost of grief: 'Blood men too. I see Richard One-eye. I see Ratty.'

'Is Keech there?' Duro said.

'No Keech.' He stepped away from the fallen board. 'Careful. Burrows men have sharp eyes.'

Xantee and Duro looked out. The first thing they saw was a brown pond with rushes at the edge. Hari had swum there, escaping from the Whips. It was smaller than Xantee had imagined, or maybe it had shrunk since that time. The statue of Cowl the Liberator was smaller too. His mouth seemed wide in grief rather than victory. His chest and shoulders grew moss and a curtain of sun-dried weed hung from his raised sword. A black and white gull was perched on his head, but it flew away squawking when Xantee said, Get away from here. There are better places than here.

Keech's men were close below. She picked out the one called Ratty (rat was in his twitching nose), and Richard One-eye. They had been Blood men but seemed no different from the others: barefooted, splay-footed, clad in string-stitched trousers and leather jerkins bald at the shoulder blades. There were no women. Keech must have broken the bands of knife-women Hari had told her of and returned them to their 'proper' place, which was cooking, she supposed, and sex and breeding. The men below her, resting on the cobbled stones where the Whips had herded their captives, smoking some sort of weed that sent a dung stink into the air, playing a game with wooden dice, cursing, laughing, looked as if women had never entered their lives. Yet if they caught her . . . Xantee could not finish the thought, but stepped back and let Tarl take her place.

'You've seen them. Let's go,' she said.

'I'm waiting for Keech.'

'Why do you need him?'

'Quiet, girl.'

'Why?'

One of the dogs growled softly, but after a moment Tarl answered, 'To find out.'

'Find out what?'

He turned and looked at her. 'If I need to kill him.'

She did not understand. When he turned away again she risked going into his mind, smoothly, like a sleeve of Dweller silk sliding on skin. He shifted his shoulders, troubled, not knowing why, then came away from the window and sat down by the wall.

'Watch, boy,' he said to Duro. He closed his eyes to sleep, but Xantee, still soft, kept his thoughts in motion. She found Keech there: a short man, bandy-legged but heavy in his torso. He had a blind milky eye and a lopsided face. Tarl was afraid of him. It surprised her. She had supposed he was frightened of nothing. He feared – she could barely find it – a darkness, a power, in Keech's mind. She risked going deeper to find what it was, but Tarl's eyes flew open and fastened on her, and the dogs, which had lain down at his sides, rose to their feet, growling.

'What games are you playing, girl?' Tarl said.

'I was trying to help you sleep,' she lied.

'I don't need help. Keep away.'

'Yes. I'm sorry.'

The dogs sank down again and in a moment slept, and Tarl slept too.

What are you doing, Xantee? Duro said.

Finding out why he needs to see Keech.

And why's that?

I don't know. Something Keech has that Tarl doesn't have. He hates Keech and wants to kill him. But I think he'd like to follow him too.

What for?

Getting the burrows together. Making them one. Tarl would have liked to do that. He doesn't want to take Keech's place, he likes dogs more than people, but he likes the way Keech has kept the burrows equal with the clerks. He doesn't want to spoil that. And he hates the Clerk more than he hates Keech. He wants to feed the Clerk to his dogs – she shuddered – like Ottmar.

Ancient history, Duro said, turning back to his spyhole.

But still, he'd like to kill Keech.

Well, he might have a chance, because he's here.

Who, Keech?

Duro gave a silent laugh. The king of the burrows, he said.

She went to his side and saw what amused him. There was nothing kinglike about the man coming round the edge of the pond. The picture she had found in Tarl's mind was accurate: bandy legs, thick chest, a blind eye like a milk-stone on a beach, a face mottled grey by disease on one side, and fallen so his cheek hung like a dewlap. He was like a dog that should slink at the rear of the pack, yet here he was leading this band of savage men, telling them when to fight and when to kill. He was dressed the same as them. So, Xantee thought, it's in his mind, it's in his tongue.

He was white-haired, and white in the half of his beard that grew, and older than the man in Tarl's mind. He moved as though his joints rasped, one bone against the other. But his good eye was as quick as a beetle. He carried a sword of hammered iron in his hand.

The men lounging on the cobbles made no move to rise. Keech was not that sort of king. He made his way from the western gate past the edge of the pond, paused to spit in the water, whacked a biting insect from his face, quick as a cat. No sign of sore joints in that movement. He ran his sword into its sheath, unstrapped his belt and dropped it, sat down with the dicing men and started to play. A scout crept close to him and whispered. Keech stopped the game by putting his hand on the thrown dice – his first sign of command. He listened, nodded, and the man edged away. The game went on. Another scout arrived and reported, then a third. The sun sank low and shadows crept along the cobblestones from the western side of the square.

Tarl woke and the dogs were instantly on their feet.

'Keech is here,' Duro said.

'Why didn't you wake me, boy?' He pulled Duro from the spyhole and took his place, then made a puff of breath, more puzzled than aggressive. 'Keech,' he said. The dogs had their noses to the lower hole again. Xantee and Duro eased them away, using a pressure that would not antagonise them, and knelt side by side, looking out. There was Keech playing dice, his hands as quick as snakes. Xantee felt the power of the man. She sensed the darkness in him. Duro's shoulder, hard against her, his cheek touching hers, softened her fear; but still Keech held her. Something moved in him, deep in his mind, like the shadow of a giant fish deep in the sea.

Duro, don't go there, she said, meaning don't try to penetrate Keech's mind.

No, he said.

I think he'll know.

Tarl stayed at the spyhole, muttering to himself and fingering his knife. Xantee knelt back from the hole and read his thoughts, and found confusion. Hatred of Keech. Admiration too.

'Yes, girl,' Tarl said, glancing down at her. 'Keech is the burrows. Keech is king.'

'If we stay here he'll find us,' she said. She felt the truth of it: some combination of senses – smell, hearing, sight, and some other sense, rising from the darkness in him – would point the man in their direction.

She looked out again and saw women emerging from the western gate. They carried bags of meat and open pots of steaming greens and put them down among the resting men. Two of them lowered a bag and pot in the circle of dice players. Keech drew a haunch of meat out of the bag – good meat, this, from some forest animal. He dipped into the pot and took a dripping handful of greens. It must have burned him for he gave a grunt of pain. One of the women laughed and he snarled at her, then grinned with the half-mouth in the good side of his face. The men ate. The women waited.

Xantee, Duro said, it's Hans. It's the man we caught.

He had come through the south gate and was slinking round the edge of the pond. He approached Keech and stood behind him, and Keech beckoned without looking round.

Hans crouched and whispered in his ear. Xantee could not hear what he was saying, but she read Keech's disbelief in the sudden stiffening of his shoulders. He swung his head and looked at Hans. The man reeled back as if he had been struck.

'Lies,' Keech roared.

Hans fell to his knees.

'This man is lying to me. Hold him.'

Two men sprang at Hans and jerked him to his feet. Keech rose slowly. But instead of reaching for his knife, as Xantee had feared, he took Hans's jaw in his hand and forced his face upwards.

'Look at me, Hans.' He spoke softly but his voice travelled clearly in the silence that had fallen on the square.

'Now, what did you see?'

'Nothing, Keech. I swear it. Empty streets, that's all.'

'And what do you see now?'

'I see you, Keech.'

'And who do you fear?'

Hans writhed but the men held him.

'I fear you, Keech.'

Keech smiled. His good eye, sharp as a blackthorn, pierced Hans.

'Then tell me what you saw.'

'Keech, I saw . . .'

'Tell me.'

'I saw . . .'

'It's easy, Hans. Just turn around and face the other way.'

The men who held Hans began to turn him, but Keech hissed angrily. He meant something else.

Duro, he's breaking into his mind, Xantee said.

'Now,' Keech said.

'Keech, I saw dog marks in the street. And I heard . . .'

'What did you hear?'

'A voice.'

'Where from?'

'In my head. I don't know where from.'

'A man's voice?'

'No, a woman's. A girl's.'

'What did she say to you, Hans?'

'She said – she asked – if Keech knows Tarl has come.'

'Tarl?'

'The dogman, Keech.'

'I know who he is. So he's here. The women who saw him were right. With two dogs. And a boy and girl. The girl is the one who spoke to you. What else did she say?'

'She asked where I would go to report.'

'And you said People's Square?'

'Yes, Keech.'

Keech put his hand in his beard. Xantee felt him thinking; felt his thoughts flick and move like tadpoles in a pond, but could not make out what they were. She knew if she tried to go deeper he would feel her and reach out for her. She could repel him, or at least hold him still, she was confident of it, but she could not hold sixty men, even with Duro's help.

'And you told her tonight, Hans?' Keech said.

'Her voice was in me like a hand, Keech, picking up what she wanted.'

'And mine is in you like a knife. Which is stronger?'

'Yours, Keech. Yours.'

Keech smiled – half his mouth, the other half dead. 'At the end she told you to forget?'

'Yes, Keech. Forget.'

'And what did you do?'

'I rubbed out the footprints of the dog.'

'And forgot?'

'Yes,' Hans whispered.

'But now you remember?'

'I remember.'

'Then what is the thing you will not say?'

'Nothing, Keech. Nothing.'

'Hans, you lie. Shall I dig out your lie with my knife?'

Hans began to cry and the men holding him pushed him back and forth like a child.

'Keech, it is . . .'

'Is what, my friend? Is what?'

'It is . . . the name you told us never to say.'

'Him? The Fat One? One arm? She asked about him?'

'She said – where is he?'

'And you said?'

'In the city. In Ceebeedee.'

'Why did she want to know?'

'Keech, she did not say.'

'And then?'

'She told me to forget.'

Keech signalled the men and they let Hans go. He sank to his knees. Keech turned away, fingers in his beard. Xantee felt the turmoil in his mind – hatred of Tarl and the Clerk, hatred mixed with triumph, for he saw his way. She felt him working it out, felt his mind baring ideas with a sound like clicking, as fast as a herdsman with his shears.

'So,' he said. She felt the weight of the word but could not see what it meant. He turned back to Hans.

'This man is no use to me any more.'

The two who had held him drew their knives.

128

'No,' Keech said. 'He has turned into a girl. Go with the women, Hans. You can live with the women now.'

'Keech,' Hans pleaded.

'Go,' he said. Hans stood up and felt his way blindly through the men.

Keech said, 'Carry a pot. You're a woman now. Make yourself useful.'

Hans picked up an empty pot and went through the laughing men, with women in a grinning clutch behind him. Keech raised his arm. The laughing stopped.

'Burrows men,' Keech said, 'you've heard what the girl, Hansee, says. The dogman is here. I've waited for him and he's come. Tarl, whose name was Knife in Blood Burrow. Blood Burrow is no more. We're Keech men now. But Tarl has come back with his dogs. Who wants to feast on dog meat tonight?'

The men roared with approval.

'Tarl betrayed us on the hill, when we killed Ottmar and his son. Tarl, with his son Hari, betrayed us. Now he's back and he'll die for it. And the girl he travels with, she will die. But take care, burrows men. She can wriggle like a worm into your heads. She can make you forget what you must know. So when you find her kill her quick. But Tarl, bring Tarl to me, and I will ask him why he wants to know where the Fat One is. I think, burrows men, that he has come back to betray us again.'

In the room, watching through the boards, Tarl groaned, 'No.'

'Tarl, come away. Let's get out of here. He'll find us soon,' Xantee said.

'I did not betray them. I'm burrows to the end. I'll never betray.'

'Men,' Keech said, raising his arm, this time with his knife clutched in his hand, 'soon we will hunt. We hunt tonight. We hunt the traitor, Tarl. We hunt his dogs. We hunt the girl, and the boy with her. Use your eyes. Use your noses. Sniff them out.'

The men roared again, unsheathing their knives, making them glitter in the slanting light.

'But where to start, eh? Where to go? There's a question.' Keech was almost whispering. 'Shall I tell you? We'll start here. Keech men, I smell dog. They've come to us. I smell traitor. I smell Tarl.'

Tarl stepped back from the spyhole. 'No,' he bellowed. He drew back his fist and smashed the rotten boards on the window, raining broken wood into the square. He thrust his head through the hole.

'I am Tarl. I'm not a traitor. I'm Blood Burrow,' he cried. He pushed out his arm, holding the black knife. 'Here is my knife, my knife for the burrows. Show me the Clerk, I will kill him.'

Keech gave a little spring of triumph, slapping his bare feet on the cobbles. 'Bring him to me. Kill the girl,' he shouted. His men broke around him and streamed across the square. Their rush was so sudden Xantee did not know which way to run. They scattered the retreating women, knocked Hans to the ground and trampled him.

Xantee, there must be stairs for them to get up here, Duro said. 'Tarl, which way to the stairs?'

'No stairs,' Tarl said, stepping away from the window.

'They're going to kill us. Where do we go?'

Tarl shook himself, restored himself. His eyes darted. 'They'll have to climb. Follow me.'

He ran from the room, followed by the dogs. Xantee and Duro ran after him. He led them back the way they had come, away from the corner of the square the men had rushed to. Xantee heard them shouting, making hunting cries, as they climbed the rubble to reach the floor where Tarl had smashed the window. Tarl was quick and sure, knife unsheathed, dogs at his heels. He took them along the south side, turned north the way they'd come. They reached the corner where the gatehouse stood and edged their way around the gaping hole in the floor. Cobblestones gleamed below them, and suddenly a man was there, creeping, slinking. It was the scout, Hans, who raised his eyes and saw Tarl and the dogs, and screeched, 'Here, here. The traitor is here.'

Tarl raised his knife to throw, then saw he would lose it. 'Hurry,' he cried to Xantee, and ran on.

She rounded the hole, stepping surely, with Duro behind her. Suddenly, below her, Keech came into being, like a wraith; but was fleshy, hairy, snarling, single-eyed, and stabbing into her with his mind. He was no knife-thrower or he could have killed her then, while she stood stunned by the strength of his blow. She felt Duro grab her and force her on, and his touch helped her recover.

No, she said to him – a command so strong she almost felt his arms spring away. With no pause she hurled a stronger command at Keech: Let go.

Keech staggered. He opened his mouth to call for his men, but she said: Be quiet.

He half obeyed – only half. He spoke to her: Girl, you're no match for me. I can turn you into mud.

She knew that if she weakened it was true. He would wrap her like a spider with a fly. All Hari's teaching, all Pearl's, all Tealeaf's, were concentrated in a pair of words in her mind: Believe. Act. And she heard, far off, or thought she heard, the soft singing double note of her name: Xantee.

She stared into Keech's deep black eye. He heard a voice too, she heard it say: Keech. He was strong. He would fall on her like a slide of wet clay from a mountainside. But he was slow, using his powers as though they were muscle and bone.

She knocked him over. She rolled him howling on the cobbles. She could have made him stab himself with his own knife. But she baulked at that and he had time to scream, 'Here, burrows. Here.' His black eye fastened on her again, but she closed it easily, flicked its lid shut.

See nothing, Keech, until morning.

Duro forced her on. He half carried her. She had used all her strength. All she wanted to do was lie down against a wall and sleep.

Keep going, Xantee, Duro commanded. He was putting strength in her, was moving her legs and keeping her eyes open. Tarl ran on ahead. She saw him dimly, saw the dogs like shadows at his side. He waited at a beam that climbed across a hole where water glimmered deep down.

'Are they coming?'

'They're coming,' Duro said. Xantee heard cries, heard bare feet slapping on stone floors. It seemed far off, but as her mind recovered, she understood it was close, no more than a corridor away.

132

'Tarl, where are we going?' Duro said.

'We're running, boy. That's all,' Tarl said.

'They're going to catch us.'

'Then some of them will die.'

'So will we.'

No, Xantee thought, not till Hari lives. She still had him in her mind from her encounter with Keech. He seemed to whisper but she could not make out the words. Maybe they were no more than: Run. Hide.

'Run,' she said. 'Hide.'

They climbed the beam and went through a series of rooms, crawling on rubble that mounted to gaps barely wide enough to squeeze through. Their hunters followed. Always they were closer, using their eyes like cats and their noses like dogs.

Tarl seized Her and leapt from a broken floor into the dark. He called Him and it leapt. Xantee heard it yelp.

'Girl, come.'

Xantee leapt blindly, bracing herself for impact with a floor she could not see. It jarred her but she stayed on her feet and heard Duro land beside her. They ran again, in deeper shadow, then slowed to feel their way. Xantee heard their pursuers yelling as they leaped into the dark.

'Tarl, where are we going?'

'We're in Keg. I don't know.'

'Quiet,' Duro said. Repeated it to Xantee: Quiet. A voice.

She heard it calling, hard but silent, in her head. Xantee, it said, Duro. Follow me.

Who?

I don't know. But it knows our names, Duro said.

Xantee, follow. Duro, follow. Bring Tarl and the dogs.

Behind them the slapping feet drew near.

'I'll fight them here,' Tarl said.

'No, Tarl, follow us. There's someone calling.'

'What, boy?'

'Follow.'

Duro took Xantee's arm and ran. She did not know where to, but the voice was constant, guiding them: Turn, jump, follow. There was no light in the ruins except starlight shining through broken roofs. They turned, then almost doubled back, and seemed for a time to move parallel to the chasing men.

At the next turn crawl through the hole in the wall, said the voice.

They saw it, an opening scarcely larger than an oven door.

Xantee, you, Duro said, pushing her. She crawled on sharp stones, scraping her knees, and came upright in a narrow room. A man stood beside her, holding a torch of wood that burned with a sooty flame. He pulled her out of the way as Duro appeared. The dogs came out, then turned and tried to go back. On the other side of the hole, Xantee heard a man cry out in pain and heard Tarl yell his fighting yell.

Stay, the man commanded the dogs. They fell still. Tarl, come, he said. It was a command stronger than any Xantee had ever heard, almost as strong as Blossom and Hubert might make. Tarl crawled out of the hole and stood up blindly. The man thrust his torch into Duro's hand. He sprang forward and swung on a giant slab of stone. It moved down slowly, grinding as it came. Then it sped and slipped into place with a jarring thud, closing the hole they had crawled through. They heard thin cries on the other side, then the sound of knives chipping stone.

It'll take them all night to break that down, the man said. The dogs were sniffing him. He touched their heads.

Who are you? Xantee said.

No one you know.

She saw his eyes shine green in the torchlight.

A Dweller, she said.

Yes, a Dweller. Now follow me again. We'll talk when we've put these men behind us.

He led them into the ruins, in buildings and streets and basements, and deep into the night, until Xantee thought the burrows had no end. Then she smelled the sea.

We're in Port, she said.

Yes, Port, the Dweller said. He led them on a crumbling road beside the harbour, then into a hidden place beneath a wharf. A dinghy was tied up and he ushered them in.

Xantee and Duro sat in the bow, Tarl and the dogs in the stern. Tarl had recovered.

'Where are you taking us, Dweller?'

'To a safe place,' the Dweller said. He pushed the boat out, took oars and started to row.

'There?' Tarl said, pointing at a dark shape against the starlit sky.

'Yes, there.'

It was a shed raised on piles, standing in the harbour. Once it had been part of a wharf but the decking had fallen, turning the shed into an island. The Dweller rowed towards it with easy strokes. Duro had taken the torch again, and suddenly Tarl leaned past the Dweller and seized it, making the boat tip and the dogs whine nervously. He held it close to the Dweller, forcing him to lean back.

'I know you,' he said.

'Yes, we met long ago,' the Dweller said. His three-fingered hands rested easy on the oars. He let Tarl study his face.

'You're the boy who came with Hari to Deep Salt.'

'Long ago,' the Dweller said, smiling.

'So,' Tarl said, narrow-eyed, gritting out his words as though they hurt, 'you came in that place with Hari and called me out.'

'Hari called you,' the Dweller said.

Tarl shook his head. 'You were the guide. Danatok is your name.'

'I'm Danatok,' the Dweller said.

'Then I thank you,' Tarl gritted. Xantee saw how difficult gratitude was for him.

She spoke to Danatok: Hari is my father.

I know. Now, let me row. I've got food and shelter for you.

They reached the shed on piles. Duro climbed an iron ladder to the deck running round its sides. Tarl handed up the dogs then Xantee climbed, followed by Tarl. Danatok tied the dinghy. He tossed another rope to Duro, telling him to pull. Duro hauled up a dripping cage with a dozen fish flapping inside.

'Tarl,' Danatok said, 'help me get these ready. Your dogs can eat too. Xantee and Duro, go inside. Your friends are waiting.'

Friends? Xantee said, but he made no explanation.

She found a door on the seaward side of the shed and entered a large room with bunks against the walls, a table and chairs in the centre, and a fire burning in the open grate of an iron stove. Two people were sitting in front of it, holding hands. They looked at Xantee, unsmiling.

He said he would bring you, one of them said.

Sal, Mond, Xantee said. You're alive.

TEN

They had walked through jungles and climbed over mountains and crossed plains, taking the straightest route they could find. The people with no name helped in the jungles, but in the mountains they froze and nearly died and on the plains their double strength had been barely enough to keep fangcats away. They arrived in the city four days before Xantee and Duro. Danatok found them hiding at the edge of the burrows and took them to his home on the harbour.

We've come to kill the gool, Sal and Mond said.

They had no idea where the gool mother might be. They had met no gool on their way.

But, they said to Xantee, when you find her, tell us and we'll come to fight.

Danatok's story took longer. He told it as the travellers ate fish baked in the oven and drank tea brewed from the bitter leaves of weeds that grew in the wasted streets of Port. He had lain in the Dweller sickhouse for many weeks after saving Tarl and it was a year before his strength returned. But he would never have to go back to Deep Salt and that knowledge helped him recover. His body grew strong. His mind was changed. Lying in the sickhouse, he had learned to love solitude. After working in the gardens all spring and sailing out with the fishermen in summer, he left Stone Creek. For many years he lived alone in the forests that stretched as far as the Inland Sea. He learned the languages of birds and animals. He learned the language of the earth, of trees, of streams, of flowers. Sometimes he thought he might change flesh with the earth and become part of it. The voice that spoke his name became a familiar sound, like a bird calling: Danatok. He asked it no questions. He swallowed it like water and it lay silent in him until it spoke again. He knew it had nothing more to say and that he had no more to learn.

'Xantee, you've heard the voice? Duro, you've heard?' He spoke aloud so Tarl would hear.

'Yes,' they said.

'Tarl, you could hear if you weren't so busy,' Danatok said.

'I talk with dogs. That's enough for me,' Tarl growled.

Danatok smiled. He went on with his story. Told how, at the jungle edge, he had met, but not seen, the people with no name. They had become his familiars. They taught him jungle skills – medicines, tracking, survival. After many years, they taught him how to sing so that dangerous animals could be pushed away.

'But I could push them already, with my mind,' Danatok said.

They showed him how to draw down light from the sky and store it in himself and make it live again in the night.

'I can do that, but it's hard, so I don't try very often. I have to sleep for days afterwards.'

Danatok perfected his own skills. He learned to speak more clearly and at a greater distance than any Dweller had ever managed before. And he could know, if he chose, whatever was in a Dweller's or a human's mind.

'You know I'd like more fish, then,' Tarl said.

'Help yourself,' Danatok said.

'When did you find out about the gool?' Xantee said.

'Yes. The gool. I went back to live in the village, but soon I knew I could never stay. I needed the forest and needed to be alone. So I left again and the people with no name called me to the jungle's edge. They showed me a gool that had slid from a crack at the bottom of a cliff beside a swamp. It was like a blob of spit a sick cow coughs up. They had tied it in threads of thought stronger than iron. I looked into it and couldn't find anything there. No life I could recognise. But it was alive, with tiny organs turning over under its skin, and a tiny eye like a fish scale.'

He flicked a scale off the table edge.

'It looked out from its world and struggled to get into ours.'

'What is it? The gool?' Duro said.

'I don't know,' Danatok said. 'It stank like a dead whale on a beach. Then the people took me to one they'd found too late. It had grown. It was as big as – as a whale. And it was eating everything it found. They told me of others. They told me these creatures were eating the world.'

'Sal and Mond found one,' Xantee said.

The cousins nodded but did not speak.

'Hari saved them. But it wrapped one of its arms around his neck and it won't let go.'

'I've talked with Blossom and Hubert,' Danatok said. 'Hari grows weaker every day. But he breathes. His heart beats. His blood flows. And Pearl sits by his side. There's still hope.'

'How do you talk with the twins?' Duro said.

'They're far away. Their voices are as thin as a tree-bat's cry and I have to lie as still as a bear in his winter sleep. But the twins have the voice inside helping them and when they speak, "Blossom" and "Hubert" mingle with "Danatok", so we hear.'

'And Hari lives,' Xantee said. 'I knew. I would have felt it if he'd died.' She wiped tears from her eyes. 'Did they say anything about Lo?'

'He stays with the people with no name, that's all they know.'

Tarl sucked the last flesh from the head of a fish and laid it down. He wiped his fingers in his beard. 'So my son sleeps on a bed, where he's no good to anyone. How do we get this thing off his neck and turn him back into a man?'

'By finding the red star and the white and killing them,' Xantee said. 'When they died the gool in Barni's story died too.'

'And all the other gools in the world?' Tarl said.

'I don't know. But if there's a mother gool and we find her . . .'

'I don't know this story of Barni,' Danatok said.

Xantee told it, while Tarl yawned and sucked fish meat out of his teeth. Danatok's cat eyes narrowed with concentration. When it was done, he nodded. 'I think this Barni heard the voice.'

'And I think this voice of yours talks too much,' Tarl said.

Danatok ignored him. 'How does the story lead you here?'

'Tealeaf – Tealeaf who was Xantee – says the people of Belong wrote books. They told the history of all the people in their world, before Company came and destroyed Belong. We travelled here . . .' She stopped, realising suddenly how hopeless their search was: a lost library in a ruined city, a book that told the history of a tribe of fisherpeople on a distant coast a thousand years ago. And even if they found it . . .

'You're searching for a book that will say what the red star and the white really are?'

Yes, she whispered silently.

Xantee, Danatok said, don't give up. We'll start tomorrow. If Hari can be saved we'll save him. If this thing that eats the world . . . He stopped and thought a while, then spoke aloud, to include Tarl: 'Like you I came here searching for the gool. Dwellers watched Belong after Ottmar died. They watched while Keech and the Clerk set up their little kingdoms, then they left, believing things would stay the same for many years – a new Keech when Keech was dead, a new Clerk after the Clerk, and others of the same kind after them. So the watchers left. A cloud had sunk down on the city, and the burrows too, and Dwellers couldn't live under it. Do you feel the cloud pressing on your skin? Do you feel how it seeps into your pores and your blood?'

'We saw it from the mountains,' Duro said. 'But I can't see it now.'

'It's here. It squats on everything. I can scarcely breathe for it sometimes.'

'Is it the gool?'

'The people with no name believe it is. They can't live away from their jungle but they sense this thing.'

'There's no smell of it,' Xantee said.

'Then she's found a way to hide her smell.'

'And that's why you came, searching for the gool?'

'Yes. Keech and the Clerk are not important.'

'But Keech hears a voice,' Xantee said. 'He can "speak".'

'He hears the voice from the other side. Hari heard it once. He blocked his ears. Keech listens. So does the Clerk. I've questioned men from Ceebeedee. They say he can make people scream with pain. He can make them burn as though their bones are on fire. That means the voice. But he'll die when his time comes, as we die. The gool . . .' His face contorted with the fear he had concealed until then. 'The gool will live forever.'

'How long have you been here? Have you found her?' Duro said.

'Not long enough. I've searched the burrows. I know every hole. That's how I know where to hide from Keech's men. I've only scouted the city, so I don't know it like the burrows. But these books – we have to find them.'

'If they exist,' Duro said.

'If they exist.'

'Tarl says there's a park Hari found, full of broken statues,' Xantee said. 'There's a building called Art Hall and one called Music Hall.'

'I know it,' Danatok said. 'Tomorrow we'll go there. But now . . .'

He showed them where to unroll their sleeping mats. With Him and Her snoring in front of the stove, Sal and

Mond side by side in a corner, and Tarl lying dog-like under a bunk instead of on top, there was plenty of room, but soon the shed was too hot and smelly for Xantee. She felt as if the walls were leaning in and the cloud that enveloped the city had seeped through the roof. She rose quietly from her bunk and carried her sleeping mat out to the deck, leaving the door ajar. The dogs looked up but made no sound. Danatok, awake on his bunk, said, Sleep well.

She made no reply. She did not want anyone in her mind. She laid her mat on the west-facing deck so nothing stood between her and the sea. The water was black, with glints of gold that made it seem like velvet, but it was the sky that took her breath away. It was littered with stars, flung out as though by a sower scattering seed – stars white and red and yellow and blue, and constellations, all the familiar swords and trees and necklaces and cooking pots Pearl had taught her to recognise. Oh yes, she thought, feeling the vastness swallow her, and taking, in turn, the vastness into herself. She waited for her name to be spoken and smiled when it was not, understanding that it was no longer necessary.

After a while Duro came out and leaned on the rail at her side. He said nothing, but stared at the stars, and she heard him catch his breath as he too was invaded by them, and by the sea. She felt his arm warm against her own and after a moment stood on her toes and kissed his cheek. Then she lay on her mat and closed her eyes. Duro went inside for his own mat and lay down with his head almost touching hers and his feet pointing away. They slept till dawn.

ELEVEN

Dried fish and more of the bitter tea for breakfast. Then they rowed ashore, leaving Sal and Mond in the shed. The smaller their group the better chance they had of moving in the burrows unseen. Tarl, walking behind them through the streets of Port, soon grew impatient. Danatok knew this part of old Belong better than he – besides, Tarl did not believe in a library and books. He called the dogs from their scouting.

'I'm going this way,' he said, indicating a street that turned towards the burrows. 'I'm going to have a look at the Clerk.'

'Tarl, they'll catch you,' Xantee said.

'I know some hiding places.'

'Not in the city. You've never been there.'

'Then I'll learn,' he said. 'Goodbye, girl.'

He turned, with Him and Her at his side, and was gone. Xantee felt she would never see him again. He had not felt like kin, yet he was Hari's father and she was sorry to see him go. She wished she had left him safe in the forest – the Dog King with his dogs.

Danatok led, keeping close to the water. Although many of the buildings were less damaged in this part of Belong, they met no people and Xantee began to understand how the population of the burrows had thinned since Hari's time. Many people had fled into the country. Many had died from starvation, disease, war, murder. She wondered if the gool's hunger was really much worse than the hunger of humans that led them into so many disasters.

By mid-morning they reached the park with the broken statues. Trees had grown out of the shattered marble. Their roots twined round heads, arms, torsos, making another sort of sculpture – roots like arms themselves, roots like grabfish.

Here, Danatok said, speaking silently now that Tarl was gone.

He led them into the arched doorway of a building standing almost undamaged at the eastern side of the park. Carved above the door, worn by rain and windblown grit, but legible still, were the words: ART HALL. The walls were standing but the roof had collapsed. Rooms opened off a large hall where broken masonry lay everywhere. The bare walls were red with lichen and black with water stains. Xantee tried to imagine what the place had been like when Belong was a great city – paintings and tapestries on the walls (she had never seen either but thought she knew what they were), pots and jugs of baked clay and vases of blown glass (there were clay shards and glass chips in the rubble), statues carved from marble or cast in bronze so shiny your face looked back at you from some hero's shield. Pearl had told her of

145

these things hanging or standing in her home when she was a child, and that most were looted from Belong. Soldiers had scoured the ruins for everything of value after Company's Liberation War.

Xantee turned away.

We don't need to go in there.

They crossed a corner of the park, around ponds of dead water and patches of stinging weed, and stopped on the south side. The building that had stood there looked as if it had been lifted up and dropped. It lay almost flat, with spikes of masonry rising like fractured bones. The portico had toppled forward. Its columns lay criss-crossed like the limbs of the statues in the park. Duro climbed into it, looking for something that might tell what the building had been.

Here, he called.

He had come across a flat stone, part of a cross-piece that had run between two columns. Carved into it were three letters: MUS. The word broke off.

Music, Xantee said. Pearl's wooden flute made the only music she had heard – that and voices singing in the fields, and the singing of the people with no name. She could not imagine music that needed a great hall.

If there was a book hall it must have been over there, Duro said, pointing through trees obscuring the west side of the park. They made their way across another corner and found a building almost intact. It too had marble columns and a portico but if a name had been carved on it a cannon bolt had blown it away. Jagged stones littered the ground. They picked their way into the porch, alert for people who might be living in this building that still had its roof.

Silence inside, absolute stillness, until a lizard scuttled away and a rat ran up a stair-rail like an acrobat and vanished into darkness at the top. The staircase led nowhere – collapsed walls and deep hollows opened beyond. Water dripped through the ceiling from rain puddles made days ago.

There are no books here, Xantee said. And if there were . . .

Rats would have shredded them and water rotted them.

They explored every room and hollow and found a pile of parchment rolls in a basement. When they tried to unroll them the leather fell in pieces and only marks like spider legs – parts of letters, parts of words – showed on the slimy surface.

Books about weapons, Duro said. How to forge swords and spears.

But it proves this was a book hall, Xantee said.

Where are the books gone?

Looted, Danatok said. Company took everything it could sell.

So we'll never find them, Xantee said. They'd send them in ships over the sea.

They'd send the precious things. Gold and jewels. Paintings perhaps. Decorated pots. Tapestries and costumes and cloth. Those were the things Company liked – whatever made them rich. But books – they wouldn't see much value in books.

They still took them.

My father, Duro began. He was silent a moment. My father told my mother . . .

Yes, what?

He worked in Ottmar's salt warehouse. There was a room at the back where the men sat to eat their cheese and bread. Ten minutes, enough for a crust and a mouthful of water and a piss, then the foreman was shouting at them . . .

Duro, what? Xantee said.

They sat on rolls of – he didn't know what they were – thin leather, he said, rolled on sticks. With marks on the leather. My father smuggled one home in his trouser leg. He and Tilly used it for firewood, in the stove.

Books, Xantee said. But why didn't you tell us before?

We were looking for a library.

And these were stored in the backroom of a warehouse, Danatok said.

Duro, can you take us there?

I wasn't born. Anyway, what chance of them still being there? And, if they are, what chance of them being the ones we want – if the ones we want were ever written?

Xantee held a piece of damp parchment in her hand. There was one word on it, written in a script with curling ends making it almost impossible to read. *Arrow*, it said. Should she take it as a message: go where the arrow flies, follow Duro's memory of his mother's story? Why not? They had nothing else.

Danatok, she said, can you take us into the city?

Yes. It's time I had a better look at it. I've seen Keech. Now it's time to see the Clerk.

It's the gool we want, not the Clerk, Duro said sourly.

Well, perhaps she's in the city. We can go the way Tarl went.

How?

It's another thing the people taught me, how to follow animals by their scent. We'll follow the dogs.

They left the Book Hall, with its empty rooms and dripping ceiling and went back along the waterfront. Danatok untied the dinghy from its mooring under the wharf and they rowed to the shed for more supplies – water, dried fish, flat bread he had baked from root flour. Sal and Mond made ready to come with them.

We want to hunt for the gool. We can feel her.

Where? Xantee said.

Everywhere.

They would say no more than that and, once ashore, they refused to travel with Danatok into Port but made off without a word into the burrows. Xantee wasn't sorry to see them go. She found their locked hands disturbing and their silence unnatural. She knew she should be responsible for them (it was what Hari would expect), but she had no mind for anything except her hunt for books – for the red star and the white.

Danatok followed the scent of the dogs, and Xantee and Duro picked it up faintly too. It led them all afternoon, through Port and into the winding streets of Bawdhouse Burrow. They met no people and saw only a single rat scuttling into a drain. When night came they slept in a sheltered yard below the city wall. The dog scent was fainter in the morning. Xantee and Duro lost it but Danatok kept heading westwards, back towards the sea.

Here, he said, stopping at the mouth of a drain in the base of the wall. The opening was head high and the ceiling had fallen but the dog scent led nowhere else. Tarl must have found a way through.

Duro, this is where Pearl and Hari came to steal the salt, Xantee said.

Memory of her parents was keeping her strong. She would be terrified without them – and again the thought of Hari dying turned her muscles to water.

Come on, Xantee, Duro said.

He was a help too. And memory of the starry sky and the velvet waves was a help. She followed Danatok into the drain. He found a way round and over mounds of fallen stone. Xantee felt his pain as he made light, drew it from inside himself as the people had taught him. Tarl must have made a torch or trusted to the noses of the dogs. But soon light flooded from a hole in the ceiling. Fallen earth made a hill for them to climb. The dog scent led them, paw-marks too, and Tarl's footprints, in the loose earth. They emerged in a street so wide it made them feel like beetles on a table-top. It seemed impossible that with so many undamaged buildings no one was about. They ran for the nearest doorway. Tarl had done the same. The dog smell was there.

We don't need to follow him any more, Xantee said. He's looking for the Clerk. We're looking for Ottmar's salt warehouse.

I'm looking for the Clerk too, Danatok said.

Later, Xantee said.

He smiled at her, amused at the way she had taken charge.

The warehouses are that way, he said, pointing. We'll have to go around Ceebeedee.

Then let's go.

Send your minds well in advance. The Clerk's men have crossbows.

I thought they'd have bolt guns, Duro said.

The technology's lost. The cannons are tipped over in the squares. The gas lamps are broken. The steam engines rust in the yards. Nothing's made any more. Men live in the

buildings as though they're caves. The Clerk is king of a
thousand ragged men.

Where does he have his headquarters? Duro said.

In Ceebeedee, where Ottmar had his. We can go along
the edge.

It took them the rest of the day. The buildings of
Ceebeedee, many pocked with cannon holes from the wars
– Ottmar against the clerks, the clerks against the workers,
the burrows against everyone – stood white in the midday
sun, then turned pink as it went down. Danatok took them
through railway yards with rusting rails and engines marked
on their sides with the faded emblem of Company, the Open
Hand. They camped for the night in an empty shed, and in
the morning followed the rails into a district of warehouses.
All had been looted years ago. They stood dark and empty
and echoing. People had lived in some. Ashes lay caked on
the floors, hardened into stone. Bones were scattered about
– always bones. The skeleton of a Whip was propped in a
doorway, rusty bolt gun in his hand. It was someone's joke
but Xantee felt sick. A fog of cruelty seemed to lie over the
city; and with it the invisible weight of the gool.

Ottmar, Duro said.

She looked where he pointed, half expecting to see the
man, but it was a name in flaking paint over wide double
doors with rails leading into them. OTTMAR SALT: she
shivered as she read. Ottmar was the man her mother Pearl
had fled from. He had thrown Pearl's family – and all the
Families – from the cliffs. He had made himself king. He
had planned to use the green salt to poison his enemies. He
had killed and tortured. And then Tarl's dogs had killed him.

151

The dreadful story made her harden her lips to keep from shrieking.

Duro put his arm around her shoulders. She shook it off. There was no comfort for such pain and cruelty.

They went through the double doors to the place where the rails ended. Wagons had loaded salt from a wooden floor five steps high. There were no wagons now, just emptiness and shadows. They climbed the steps. Grains of salt, brown with age, gritted under their feet. At the far end of the huge shed a row of windows high in the wall let in enough light for them to advance.

'My father,' Duro said, aloud. He was almost crying. 'My father worked here. All his life.' Xantee tried to take his hand, but he too wanted no comfort. 'You only get one life and he spent all his here so Ottmar could get fat.'

They went deep into the shed, to a stone floor where salt-cake had been broken with hammers. A heavy wooden door stood in the end wall. The bolt was twisted off but the door was latched with a length of iron pipe. Duro wrenched it out. The door scraped on the stone floor as he pushed it open. The room beyond was airless, windowless, and empty except for rubbish piled against the back wall.

Nothing, he said.

Books, Xantee said, approaching the rubbish.

They were as round as rolling pins and stacked like firewood. Pieces of leather poked out like tongues. They bent and cracked as she eased out a roll and laid it on the floor. But when she tried to open the parchment it broke into pieces in her hand.

It's no good, Xantee. They must have been here a hundred years, Duro said.

How did Ottmar get them?

Maybe they were stored in this shed before he used it as a warehouse. He must have thought they weren't worth anything, so he left them.

And we can't read them, she said. She tried to unroll the parchment again but it broke like the hard bread Danatok had baked, and broke again with each renewed pressure of her hand.

Books were never going to help us, Duro said.

Danatok walked along the stacked rolls.

The workmen sat here, he said, stopping at a place where the stack had been lowered to form a knee-high bench. See how they're flattened. They make a good seat.

My father sat here, Duro said wonderingly.

Carefully he lowered himself on to the books. Xantee expected them to break in pieces, but instead they gave a groan as his weight forced them down.

These ones are softer, he said, feeling the leather. He brushed his hands. Salt, he said. My father came home covered in salt. It was in his clothes and hair. Tilly said she used to make him shake it on the table and she'd sweep it up and use it for the stew. So here . . .

It fell out of the men's clothes when they sat down, Xantee said. And it's kept these books from rotting away.

She pulled out the book Duro had rested his hand on. The outer part was softer than the layers inside. It unrolled two turns before the leather cracked. She took it out to the stone floor and put it in the light from the windows.

Can you read it? Duro said.

Just. This bit's about how to roast an ox. What herbs to use. It's a cookbook.

No wonder Ottmar thought they weren't worth anything. Xantee, the chances of finding a book about the two stars – they're nil.

We didn't come here just to walk away. Bring out some more.

Danatok kept watch. Duro carried out books one by one. Xantee unrolled them far enough to find what they were about. Some had titles painted on the outside. She did not need to unroll those. Others were less well-preserved than the book about roasting oxen, but she was able to read enough to discover the subjects. There was a book about waterwheels, a book about sowing crops, a book about the seasons, a book about the punishments allowed by law. One seemed to be about travel in foreign lands, another about the mapping of the eastern coast. Those two made her heart race. She felt she was getting close. But nothing was said about the Fish People and nothing about Barni and the stars.

The bench that had made the workers' resting place shrank to ankle height as she worked. The books close to the bottom were less well-preserved than those on top. Some unrolled only an inch before the leather snapped. Others would not unroll at all. Duro sliced them open with his knife. Deep inside, some of the words were legible. There seemed to be no order in the subjects: trade, weights and measures, cooperage, etiquette, husbandry. One seemed to be a history of Belong. One was a tale of ancient gods. Xantee kept on. If they had all been on one subject she would have grown discouraged, but in this mix of books there was a chance . . .

Eat, Xantee, Duro said as darkness invaded the shed. He made a fire of leather scraps on the stone floor.

Sleep, he said at midnight.

She lay on her mat, staring into the dark. When she slept her dreams were of words floating by, their spiky script like crows' feet, the leather they were written on flapping like bat wings.

Danatok scouted in the morning. He brought back a report of men – the Clerk's fighting men – drifting in from their homes to the centre of Ceebeedee. There seemed to be nothing in their minds except the promise of entertainment.

Did you smell the dogs? Did you find Tarl? Duro said.

He shook his head.

Duro, bring out more books, Xantee said.

What do we do when we've finished, start a school?

She made no reply. Her last dream was vivid in her mind. It was of a black man, with a traveller's cape flung back from his shoulders, sitting on stone steps leading down to the sea. He dipped a goose-quill pen in a pot of ink and wrote words on a roll of parchment held on his knee. Below him, in a moored fishing boat, a grizzled old man – a brown man, this one – was mending nets. He spoke in a language Xantee could not understand. The traveller wrote. She saw words form at the point of his pen, written in a language she knew. *Barni led us*, the traveller wrote. Duro's hand on her shoulder woke her then.

Get more books, she repeated.

He sighed and touched her head.

Your eyes are red, your face is dirty, your hair's like the backside of a sheep. When we get back to the sea I'm going to wash you.

Please, Duro, just bring them, she said.

He carried them out two by two. Half the morning went

by. Books on the early history of Belong, when it had been a fishing village. A book that went even further back, telling how the village had been founded by a poor herdsman and his wife, who found a dolphin stranded on the beach and returned it to the sea. Leave your goats and farm the sea, the dolphin said, and I will drive cod into your nets.

Duro, these are stories like Barni and the stars, she said.

We want true stories not made up ones, he replied. And there's only one row of books left. They're covered in salt.

Bring them.

He shook them free of the grains and laid them beside her. They opened more easily, but one, two, three, four – they were about ship-building, the rules of an elaborate card game, the preparation of marble for sculpture, and the practice of midwifery. Then, late in the morning, Duro came running out with a book lying across his hands like an offering.

Xantee, look here, look at the title.

She strained her eyes to see the name painted on the dark outer stick.

The history, she read slowly.

The History and Legends of the Fish People. Careful, it's brittle, don't break it.

Her hands were trembling with tiredness, her fingertips stinging with salt.

You do it, she told him.

It took him the rest of the day to break the parchment open and lay it on the floor. It was like fitting a shattered plate together. Some pieces were the size of his hand, others no larger than his fingernail. The words were tiny. Many had faded to shadows, others stayed black. They swarmed like ants in front of Xantee's eyes. She rubbed the lids and was stung so painfully by salt she cried out. Danatok came from keeping watch and made more light to help her.

Slowly she ran her eyes along the lines of words. Parchment must have been in short supply. The scribe had cramped his words together. Sometimes they collided and ran over the top of each other. She realised they were notes put down to make a later story. There was a bit about the wondrous herring catches of the settlement's early years. Then an account of a war fought with pirates. Then the building of a sea wall. These events seemed hundreds of years apart. Then – it made her cry out with delight – the story of Barni. The name splashed out of the text like a fish from water. She hooked it with her mind, dragged it free, then ran her eyes along the lines surrounding it. Barni was more than a simple fisherman. He was chief of the village council. He had led the village in its resistance to the rule of rival kings, one in the north, the other inland, who claimed the coastal lands as their own. The Fish People fought the invaders off. The kings arranged a meeting (they were the rulers of a tribe of red-skinned people in the north and a white-skinned tribe from the mountains). Each was proud, ambitious, and eager to crush the other, and each was full of malice and deceit and cruelty. They met and spoke honeyed words, while each seethed with hatred underneath. They agreed to join their armies and attack the Fish People in the next fighting season, then went their ways, each scheming to murder the other and take all the spoils for himself. Barni was aware of it. All winter long he thought and planned, distracted only by a sea monster that had arrived to live in a cave along the coast from the village. Men went out to slay it and were slain themselves. But Barni, playing on their fears, taught that the monster was a magical beast spawned from the hatred of the two opposing kings, and feeding on their cruelty and deceit, and so growing stronger every day, and that when the kings were slain, the red king and the white, then the monster would starve and die.

Xantee read aloud. Her voice was breathless.

Duro, it's the red star and the white. The kings are the stars. Go on, don't stop.

There were only a few more lines. She read: He assembled the best fighting men of the village and took the strongest boat and sailed north to the red king's city. Barni and his men slipped through the defences in the night and slew the king in his bed with his concubine. Then they sailed inland, up a wide river and across a lake and down another river and came to the white king's city. There they –

The parchment finished at that point.

'Oh,' Xantee cried aloud. She wanted the end of the story. She wanted to know.

Duro hunted for more books. He brought out the last of them. None went on with the story of the Fish People.

It doesn't matter, we know what happens. They kill the white king, who's the white star. The gool dies. And then, after hundreds of years, the truth turns into legend. I wish I'd known Barni.

The red star and the white were men, Xantee said.

Danatok let his light die. He sat down, exhausted.

Just as they are today, he said.

Yes, she breathed.

Duro nodded.

In the darkening shed, Xantee kneeling, Danatok sitting, Duro on his feet, they stared at each other.

Keech and the Clerk were the two stars. Keech and the Clerk had brought the gool into the world. The gool was their spawn.

TWELVE

In the morning, before the sun was up, they gathered the pieces of the Fish People book and piled them in a corner of the shed. Xantee and Duro swept up salt with their hands, the grains almost black with age and dirt, and scattered them over the parchment in an effort to preserve it. It was the best they could do. No one would read the book again. They felt they were preserving its bones.

They ate quickly, rolled their mats, and left Ottmar's warehouse. The railway track ran out of the yard and turned towards the west. They followed it in the red dawn. It fell away on a long incline to the city wall and through a gate and down to Port. Danatok turned northwards, where the buildings of Ceebeedee squatted like swamp frogs. The marble, pink in the sun, should be beautiful, the city opening like a flower, but the buildings gave the impression of having swallowed something and of waiting greedily for more.

Xantee knew where Danatok was leading them. In the

darkness of the warehouse, on their sleeping mats, they had talked and planned before dropping off to sleep. They were going to find the Clerk. They were going to kill the Clerk. They had argued into the night, but there was no other way. Xantee had wanted to talk with him, plead with him if she had to. He was a human, like them – or, at least, like Duro and her – and he would not want his world devoured by a creature from – where? From the other side of nature was the only explanation she could give. If he understood what he and Keech had done, calling the gool from wherever it lurked, giving it entry to the world, then surely he would renounce it and that might be enough to make it die.

Please, she had pleaded, let me talk to him.

Xantee, Duro said, you can't talk with people like the Clerk. He's Keech in another shape. You've seen Keech. Do you think you could talk *him* into doing anything?

No, she whispered, but . . .

In the dark, she fingered her knife and knew she could never plunge it into another person, no matter how evil he was.

If we can take control of him, she began, but Duro interrupted: Barni didn't try to talk with the red and white kings, or control them or capture them. Barni killed the buggers, that's what he did.

Danatok? Xantee pleaded.

There's no other way, the Dweller said.

She heard his pain. Dwellers took life only for food. Killing humans was as bad for him as killing his own kind. It would place him outside his tribe forever.

They had no idea how to kill the Clerk. Or kill Keech after him. And, Xantee thought, no idea if the gool would die

161

when they were dead. And where was the gool anyway?

She followed Danatok into Ceebeedee. Each time they entered a new street the great buildings in the centre had edged closer. Beyond them, across an unseen suburb, rose the hill where the mansions of the Company Families had stood. Paths zigzagged up the side as though drawn with rulers and black ink. There were scrubby trees at the top, although here and there the skeleton of a larger one stood against the sky. The mansions were gone, except for a half-hidden shape that might be House Ottmar, standing alone.

Xantee, Duro hissed.

She was walking without caution, thinking in a sick way of the Clerk, and remembering Pearl and Hari, sixteen years before, taking on a task far more difficult than hers.

What? she said.

He pulled her into a doorway where Danatok was already concealed. Men went by at the end of the street.

What do you think you're doing? Duro said.

Getting ready, she answered.

For what?

She did not know. All she knew was that it would not be killing.

Quiet, Danatok said. He was searching the minds of the men with his lightest touch.

They're going back to their homes, he said. The Clerk is sending them home.

Why?

He's kept his guards with him. Keech wants a meeting.

When?

Tomorrow. The Clerk has sent a messenger saying yes,

because . . . Danatok paused, then gave a silent groan. Because he's got Tarl. He's captured him. He wants to show him off to Keech.

Xantee turned to the wall. She put her face in her hands and felt tears seeping through her fingers. 'Tarl,' she whispered. She had not liked him. She had not felt they were of the same blood – yet now she was overwhelmed with love that started there, in her blood, in the beating of her heart.

They'll kill him, Duro said.

I can't see what the Clerk means to do. Maybe trade him with Keech for something he wants, Danatok said.

Then Keech will kill him. Did they capture the dogs?

I don't know.

It doesn't change anything. We kill the Clerk. We save Tarl. It's simple, Duro said.

No, Danatok said. We wait till tomorrow. Then we can get Keech and the Clerk together.

All right, Duro said. But we've seen Keech. I want to have a look at the Clerk and find out how strong he is. How well he can speak. Xantee, are you all right?

While we're waiting Hari might die, she thought.

We'll talk with Blossom and Hubert, Danatok said, picking up the thought. But Xantee, you'd have felt it, Hari dying. So he's alive.

Yes, she said. But each day . . .

We'll get Keech and the Clerk tomorrow, Duro said. Then the gool will die.

She turned and looked at him sadly. Duro was always straightforward, always sudden. He had not believed in Barni's story, now he followed it as if Barni had stepped out of the parchment roll and spoken in his fisherman's voice: Kill the red king and the white. Duro would try. But if the Clerk was anything like Keech Duro would fail. Then he would die and his death would hurt her even more than Hari's.

Xantee saw what she must do. She closed her mind so Duro and Danatok would hear no whisper of it.

More men passed the end of the street. Then Danatok led them to a doorway close to the intersection. He chose an old man, scaly and bent and slower than the others, and sent out a half-command: You're tired. Sit and rest. The man obeyed: sat on a step, and finding himself there, took a plug of weed from his pocket, bit off a chunk, and chewed. A young man, short-bearded, cruel-eyed, stopped and said, 'Buggered, are you, Gran'dad? Give us a bite of your weed.'

The older man handed it over and the young man bit, then spat.

'Where'd you get this muck? Call it plug? It tastes like them dogs have pissed on it.'

'Give it back, then,' the old man said.

The other dropped it and kicked it into the gutter. 'You can fight the dogs for it if you find them.' He went on. The old man chewed placidly and wiped his yellow chin.

So they haven't caught the dogs, Duro said.

Danatok searched out the old man's name.

Glubby, he said, rest a while yet. Where are you going?

'Home,' the old man said, and gave a start at the sound of his voice.

Where have you come from?

'Headquarters.'

Why did the Clerk call you in?

164

'To see the dogman in his cage.'

What will he do with the dogman?

'Show him to Keech. Then have some fun with him.'

Glubby, where's the gool?

'Don't know no gool.'

'Talking to yourself, old man? Time for the bone yard,' said a younger man, passing.

Danatok waited.

Glubby, where's headquarters?

'Trade House. Old Trade House. Underneath the bell. I used to be night watchman at Trade House. Who's asking?' He spat brown juice.

Danatok made his hold deeper.

Is the Clerk there?

'He's there.'

With how many men?

'Twelve. His guard.'

And the dogman in a cage?

'Yes, the dogman. The Clerk makes him howl.'

Where does he meet Keech tomorrow?

'On the hill. Usual place. Between Ottmar and the Hand.'

All right, Glubby. Go home now. No one's spoken to you. Remember nothing.

The old man stood up, shook himself, retrieved his plug of weed from the gutter, and walked away.

So, Danatok said, we've got till tomorrow.

Let's find Old Trade House. I want to see this Clerk, Duro said.

They started off. Xantee said nothing. She followed.

The streets were empty again, but Danatok led them carefully. The Trade House was in the centre of Ceebeedee. Like the other buildings of that quarter it was built in marble that years of neglect had mottled grey and yellow and brown. Wide shallow steps, like a fan, led between columns to timber doors as tall as those in Ottmar's salt warehouse. A smaller door, man-sized, opened in the bottom. A guard lounged in front of it, smoking a pipe.

Danatok drew back and led them along the side of the building. He stopped suddenly.

Dogs, he said.

Xantee felt them too, hiding behind a jumble of metal storage boxes thrown into an alley. She had imagined that Him and Her had run from the city, run for their forest, when Tarl was captured. She should have known better. The dogs were Tarl's children; they were tied to him the way she was tied to Hari and Pearl.

Dogs, she ordered, taking command, lie still.

She advanced, with Duro and Danatok beside her. The dogs growled softly, uncertainly, but fell quiet when she said, We're your friends. You know us. Their yellow eyes watched her. They trembled with suppressed energy.

Dogs, she said, we're going to find Tarl. Come with us.

The bitch, Her, seemed to nod. The dog, Him, advanced and after a moment touched his nose to her hand.

All right, she said. There's a guard on the door. We'll go past him and he won't remember. Follow us and make no sound.

She let Danatok lead again, although now she doubted that his mind was any quicker and stronger than hers. Since she had decided what to do she had been calmer. It made a stillness round her like the pause between a breath drawn in and released. When all this was over she would hear in the way he heard, and speak with a voice as far-reaching as his.

They found an entrance at the back of the Trade House building. Danatok held the guard still as they went through, then made him forget when it was done. Across a wide room at the end of a passage double doors, one slightly ajar, led on to the floor where the trading had been done in Company days. They felt men inside, a dozen or more – simple men, soldiers, active and cruel – and with them another, twisted away from his followers, with a darkness in his mind where there should be light, and nothing of the brutal fellowship Keech had demonstrated. This was the Clerk. Straining at him, Xantee felt his pain. The man was always in pain.

The dogs smelled Tarl and leaned at the doors but Danatok held them back. He led the way up service stairs at the side of the room, feeling for guards. They reached a sloping gallery at the back of the trading floor, which stretched away as long and wide as a holding paddock for cattle. The hundreds of desks and cabinets that had filled it in Company's time were jammed against the walls. A canopy of purple cloth was raised on poles in the centre, as lonely as a hut on a plain, and there, on a bed fat with quilts and swollen with pillows, a man slept, with a blanket tucked under his chin. He was like a baby. And like a baby he had his nurse – a gaunt woman sitting on a wooden chair at the bed-head, ready with a cloth to wipe his brow, or to wet his lips with water.

After Keech, striding on his bandy legs, darting his beetle eye, this man, the Clerk, seemed too soft, too inert, to be his rival. One hand, gripping the blanket edge, tightened with each breath, his cheeks swelled like a frog's, his lips parted as he exhaled, making a popping sound. He was in a drugged sleep (the cup stood on a table beside the bed) that cut the threads tying him to the world, yet Xantee sensed his self lying at the centre, as hard as stone, and knew he would wake in an instant if there was need. She wished he was awake now. She wanted to see him properly, and hear him, and work out how he could be approached.

Halfway between the gallery and the bed, Tarl sprawled in his cage. He too slept, but not as heavily as the Clerk. He was like a dog. A sound or movement would bring him to his feet. He still had the strip of blanket tied about his loins, but his knife sheath sloped empty across his hip. Xantee looked for the knife, and found it on the table by the Clerk's bed, beside his cup. Tarl's hand felt for it as he slept, the fingers opening and closing.

Sleep easy, Tarl, Xantee whispered, but the dogman's fingers would not lie still.

There was nothing in Tarl's cage – no food, no water. A man stood guard, holding a crossbow with its cord cranked tight. The cage – perhaps the cage Tarl had held Ottmar and Kyle-Ott in sixteen years before – was locked with a heavy padlock, and the key lay on the table with the knife. Eleven men – Xantee counted: the remainder of the Clerk's guard – knelt or stood quietly between the bed and the main doors. Like Keech's men, they played dice, one man throwing, the others placing bets with lead coins on a mat spread in the ring.

The Clerk slept, his lips popping, his hand twitching, his

mind iron hard in its quilting of drugs – and Tarl slept with his fingers feeling for his knife.

Danatok, Duro and Xantee crept out of the gallery and down the stairs.

Up here, Danatok said, leading them into another staircase, this one winding as it climbed. They went high above the roof of the Trade House building, and stopped underneath a bell sheltered by a domed roof. A frayed rope hung down, out of reach. Tilly had told them how the bell was rung each morning to signal the start of trading on the floor beneath. Pearl had heard it too, from her mansion on the hill. The bell-house was the highest point in Ceebeedee.

Xantee freed her mind, letting it join with Duro's and Danatok's. She pictured their combined thought flying like a spear out of the bell tower, over the city and plains and mountains and jungles, across the Inland Sea, to Blossom and Hubert in the farmhouse by the beach. She felt it thud into the ground and stand trembling there, and felt the twins put their hands on it and tug it free, then the image faded, their voices, clear, thin, childish, spoke in her head: Xantee, Duro, we've been waiting. Danatok, what's going on? Hari's worse. Hari's dying.

They could not keep distress out of their voices.

Tell us, Danatok began, but Xantee pushed him aside, took control of their triple-tongued voice, and spoke without her own distress breaking through: The thing, the gool, is it growing stronger?

Xantee, it's strangling him. Hari can't breathe. He draws air in as thin as a cotton thread. We breathe in his mouth. Pearl breathes. And the thing grows stronger. We loosen it,

169

we dig our thoughts underneath, but it tires us out and we fall asleep. Xantee, it's growing a cord inside itself, twisting tighter, and it mews with hunger, pulling out Hari's life. Unless you can . . . Xantee, unless you can . . .

How long? How long before Hari dies?

One day. Two. The healer says two. Tealeaf says two. They can open his throat and force in a tube for him to breathe – they'll do that in the morning – but the thing cuts off his blood as well as his breath.

Blossom, Hubert, listen. We've found where the gool feeds. We've found the red star and the white, and they . . .

She did not know how to put it.

. . . They circle close to each other and tomorrow they meet. The gool knows. Somehow she knows. She feeds on them. And that's why her – her children everywhere, the one on Hari's neck, the others in the jungles – everywhere – why they're growing stronger. But tomorrow we'll find her. I promise you, Hari. I promise you, Pearl.

She could not go on and Danatok took the voice, asking questions. Xantee withdrew. She had no message other than her promise, and no more questions to ask. Tomorrow, she had said. That was waiting too long. There was a way she must try now.

Danatok and Duro kept the voice going with two strands. They had questions, messages, and their concentration was so intense they did not feel her slip away. Quietly she went down the winding stairs. The dogs were waiting at the bottom. Lie still, she told them. Wait for Danatok. She went to the door that was ajar, drew it back, stepped through and closed it with a click.

The huge hall stretched in front of her, with the canopy and bed halfway along and the cage off to one side. The dice players were further away, intent on their game. Only the crossbow man saw her approach. He swung up his weapon.

'Wait,' she said, not trying to control him. 'I've got a message for the Clerk.'

He kept her covered, the bolt in the bow pointing at her breast.

'Clerk,' he called.

The man in the bed sat up slowly. The blanket fell away from his chest, revealing his arms. The left stayed bent, with the hand clawed under his chin, its fingers sharp as fish bones. The right was active, feeling under the pillows and coming out with glasses set in wire. He put them on his nose and his eyes swelled to the size of oysters, filling each lens.

'Who?' he said.

'She's got past the door somehow,' said the crossbow man. 'Says she's got a message.'

'Guard,' called the Clerk to the dice players, who had left their game and come to the bed. 'Cover her. Every one of you. Shoot if I say.'

Eleven more crossbows were trained on Xantee.

'Now,' said the Clerk. He licked his lips, worked his dry tongue, and the woman, the nurse, leaned forward with a water bottle, put her other hand at the back of his head, helped him drink. She wiped his lips with her cloth. He pushed her away.

'Now,' he repeated, 'girl. Who are you? What's your message?' He threw off his blanket and swung his feet to the floor. Keech had called him The Fat One, but Xantee saw it

171

had been in derision. The Clerk was wasted away. His clothes – red shirt, green trousers: the Ottmar colours – hung in folds on a frame that seemed made of sticks. His white feet turned inwards so the soles almost touched. Yellow nails shone on his toes like beads. They alone seemed healthy. His clawed hand rested under his chin. And his eyes, swimming behind his glasses, seemed blind. The woman knelt and fitted slippers on his inturned feet. She handed him a hat – or was it meant to be a crown? Xantee could not tell. He used the trappings of kingship in spite of the name he kept and she wondered if she should flatter him by kneeling.

'My message comes from far away,' she began, but found her thoughts jumbled by pressures from outside. Duro and Danatok had found that she was gone; they had come down the stairs and were in the passage outside the door. She felt Duro's panic and his urge to rush in and stand at her side, and felt Danatok restraining him. And Tarl had woken and risen to his feet. She saw him beyond the canopied bed, holding the bars of his cage, and she felt his grief – grief for her. She tried to put them aside. She locked her mind as though locking a door. There was a tiny room and she and the Clerk were inside, with no space for anyone else. She decided not to flatter him.

'Clerk,' she said, 'you live in a small world and the big world lies outside. I come from there and I've seen what's happening. A monster has been bred. Its name is gool. *Her* name is gool. She lives here, in your city.'

She felt the last sleep peel away from the Clerk, leaving his mind hard and clear. And this, she knew, was the man – not his sick body, not his pain, but his knowledge of himself and his knowledge that he ruled. He was like Keech. Yet when he spoke his voice was soft. It seemed he smiled at her.

'Continue, girl. Tell your story.'

It unnerved her. She tried to read him, but knew that if she went too deep he would be aware, and she did not want that – not yet. But she saw enough to know that he was not only cruel – crueller than Keech, because he was cold – but clever too, that he could dart and probe and discover. She cleared her mind.

'She lives here, secretly, and she feeds. And she has sent her children out into the world, where they grow – and as they grow the world shrinks. They feed on it. They come from – she comes from the other side of nature and has no place in our world. She must be sent back. Her children must die. Then the world lives. Listen, Clerk –'

He raised his hand like a child in school.

'A question, girl.'

'Yes?'

'Why should I care? Why should the Clerk care if the world dies? It has given me this.' He brought his good hand down and touched the bad. 'It has given me this city of fallen houses as my kingdom, and a thousand ragged thieves as subjects. It has given me nothing. Nothing but pain. Why should I care? I would kill the world if I could. I would need no gool.'

'But you know her?' Xantee managed to say.

'I've heard of creatures that grow and devour mountain-sides and jungles, and drink seas, and of course it interests me. I applaud them. What is the world that it should go on when I cannot? But here, the mother, living in my city? This is your

173

fantasy, girl, and I must know where you have it from. And who sent you. Did Keech send you?'

The question was so unexpected and thrown with such force, although in that same soft reasonable voice, that Xantee staggered.

'No,' she managed to say. 'I don't know Keech.'

'Lies, girl. You have his smell. There's a burrows stink on you. This meeting he asks for – what does he plan?'

'I don't know. I don't know Keech. But he's like you. He feeds the gool. Clerk, it's your hatred she feeds on, yours and his. Your cruelty and the darkness in your head. And in his. It needs two, and the darkness flashes back and forth. That's what she was born from and that's what feeds her still.'

The Clerk smiled. He laughed, and the woman at his side half-rose to her feet, the bowmen wavered. It was a sound they had never heard. 'A pretty story. I wish it was so,' said the Clerk. 'I would bring Keech to sit at my side and we would share the world between us. But girl –' his smile went away – 'you're lying still. What I must have is Keech's plan. And I think you know what it is.'

'There is no plan. I spied on Keech and ran from him. I came from beyond the jungles and mountains to ask you – to plead with you and him – go to the gool. Renounce her. Stop your hatred and cruelty. Send her home. That way you and he can be great kings, and no other way. Find her hiding place, Clerk. Do it quickly or the world dies.'

Again the Clerk laughed and again it did not last.

'Then let it,' he said. 'So long as Keech dies with it. And Tarl dies.' He touched his withered arm. 'Tarl, who did this to me. But I don't believe you, girl. We must find out what it is you hide.'

Tarl spoke then. He said, 'Xantee, don't waste your time. The Clerk is a worm. He is snake shit . . .'

And Xantee, hearing him begin, cried silently: Tarl, be quiet. He doesn't know I know you.

The Clerk heard them both. He struck as quickly as a snake: sent Tarl reeling from the bars with a mind-blow as heavy as a punch – and punched at Xantee too, to stun and hold her. She slid away from him, although she felt him scrape her mind. She let him think he held her, while she measured his strength. It was greater than Keech's because he had studied it and used it with calculation. She found that he could use it to burn and twist. His followers knew its strength. Pain was how he held them. If she fought with the Clerk she must use the whole of her mind and dodge his blows like a fan bird with a diving hawk.

'So,' said the Clerk, 'it's Tarl the girl plots with, not Keech. See girl, I can hold you. You have the voice but with you it's like some pretty bangle worn on your wrist. My voice is a hammer. If I wish to I can break you in pieces. Feel it, girl.'

She was ready for his blow and moved so it slid past her; but she staggered and cried out and clawed her throat, to convince him. She measured his range and focus – the one short, the other narrow – and knew that she could stay clear simply by stepping this way and that. And even if she met him head-on she could raise her hand and hold him off; and if she chose (she understood it with horror), if she chose she could strike him dead. She had not known the power she had. She cried out, inside herself, that she did not want it.

175

She did not want the power to kill.

'Now, girl, you understand how I can hurt you. Kneel to me and say I'm your king. The Clerk is king.'

Xantee knelt. She spoke in a voice still weak from the horror she felt: 'You are king. The Clerk is king.'

'And do you think Keech can oppose me?'

'Keech,' she said, 'Keech has the voice too. And the power. But he hasn't learned to use them like you. Clerk, king, I don't know Keech. I've seen him. He struck at me the way you strike but without your strength, and I ran and came to you –'

'But you know Tarl.'

'I met Tarl in the forest and asked him to guide me here so I could tell you about the gool, and tell Keech. But you don't listen.'

She had recovered herself. Her mind was working quickly. Tomorrow the Clerk and Keech would meet on the hill. She must be there. And Duro and Danatok would be there. They would force them – force the red star and the white – to recognise that they had brought the gool into the world, to recognise it and renounce her. The Clerk still kept his hold on her and she let him think she was in his power, but freed herself, left him her shadow, and said to Duro and Danatok outside the door: I'm all right. He can't hurt me. I think what he'll do is put me in the cage with Tarl. His men will carry me up the hill tomorrow. Keech will be there. Don't talk to me, Duro, he'll feel you. Tomorrow we'll make them both do what we want.

She felt Danatok restraining Duro. She knew what Duro's pain must be. Duro loved her, although he had not found a way of telling her.

Tomorrow, she said.

The Clerk took Tarl's knife from the table and held it up for Xantee to see. 'Tarl the dogman,' he said. 'Tarl the Knife. I chased his dogs away. I took his knife from him. See, here. See it, Tarl. I branded you once. And you threw your knife at me – this knife. You lost it that day. You stood naked, with your manhood gone. And you're naked again. Your sheath is empty.'

Tarl had risen to his feet and gripped the bars. 'I need no knife to kill you, Clerk,' he said.

The Clerk smiled. 'Idle boasts, they keep one's courage up. Tomorrow we'll see.'

'Tomorrow I'll crush your other arm.'

The Clerk snarled. It was the first time he had lost control. Xantee felt the blow he aimed at Tarl. She saw the dogman stagger and fall and lie writhing on the cage floor – saw his eyes bulge and teeth bite and his limbs twist almost to breaking point. She could not help him. She could not let the Clerk know her strength was greater than his. Tarl rolled over and over. He stood and ran blindly, bounced off the bars of the cage and fell bleeding to the floor, where he howled and whimpered.

The Clerk relaxed.

'That,' he said softly, 'is how you will die tomorrow. That is how the Clerk will pay you for this.' He tapped his clawed hand with the blade of Tarl's knife, then smiled at Xantee. 'You see what I can do, girl. I can do that to you if I choose.'

'Yes, I know,' Xantee said. She saw that his hatred of Tarl, the agony he had put him through, had drained his strength. In the end Keech, though primitive in his use of voice and command, might prove stronger. Tomorrow would show. But if she made them fight, would the gool grow stronger?

The Clerk yawned. 'Well, girl, you interrupted my sleep with your talk of monsters and I must sleep again. What tomorrow brings for you, I don't know. Perhaps I'll give you to Keech to play with. We'll see. But now –' he turned to his guards – 'lock her in the cage with the dogman. Watch her closely. She has some tricks of voice she might try on you. If you hear a whisper, shoot. Don't hesitate.' To Xantee again: 'Try nothing, girl.'

Xantee shook her head. Two of the bowmen led her to the cage. A third unlocked the padlock and thrust her inside. She went to Tarl, who was twitching and groaning on the floor; put her hand on his brow, seeing how the Clerk had hacked his hair off to expose his brand. She eased a healing current into him.

'He burned me,' Tarl whispered.

'I know. Lie still. Sleep now. You can't fight him here, but tomorrow, on the hill . . .'

Tarl slept.

Xantee sat with her back leaning on the bars. Two men kept her covered, with the cords of their bows cranked tight. She ignored them. With Duro and Danatok helping, she could escape from this cage, and take Tarl with her – but she did not choose to. Her attempt to persuade the Clerk had failed. She could not understand it – and could not understand his cruelty and hatred. That, with Keech's equal cruelty, and their rivalry and malice, had given birth to the gool and kept her fed. Keech would refuse to believe it, like the Clerk, she was sure. And even if they understood they would simply shrug. Xantee shivered. These men did not care if the world died. And both of them would rejoice if Hari died.

She would not let it happen. Tomorrow, she thought. Somehow she would find the way tomorrow. She slipped her hand inside her doublet and felt her knife in its sheath. The guards had not searched her. They had not thought a girl would carry a weapon. But the answer would not be found in weapons, not in knives. When she got the chance she would give hers to Tarl so he could defend himself. The answer lay elsewhere, perhaps inside her, in all the things she had learned from Pearl and Hari and Tealeaf and the twins.

She felt for Duro and Danatok. They had retreated to the bell tower. The dogs were hidden in the alley across the street.

Under the canopy the Clerk slept. He snored. The woman wet his lips with water. The guards, except for the two watching her, had gone back to their dice.

Keep hidden, keep silent, she whispered to Duro. Tomorrow, she whispered.

Yes, tomorrow, he whispered back. I'm here. Don't be afraid.

Xantee smiled. Oddly enough she was not concerned for herself, only for Hari, and for the world the gool and these agents of hers, Keech and the Clerk, were slowly turning inside out.

She lay down on the cage floor and rested.

THIRTEEN

The day was clear and sunny but the presence of the gool was in the air. She had no smell, unlike her children, but thickened every indrawn breath so that it slid into the lungs like an eel. The men carrying the cage, eight of them, coughed and spat and Xantee, in the cage, felt as if she had swallowed water from a drain. Tarl held the bars and spat too, aiming at the bowmen on either side. He was not afraid of them shooting him, nor afraid of the Clerk's torture. Somehow he meant to escape. And now he had a chance for, in the night, while the bowmen slept and the guards nodded beside the brazier that made the only light in the trading hall, Xantee had given him her knife. He had weighed the short slim-bladed thing in his hand and grunted with contempt, but slipped it into his sheath, where it sat hidden, blade and handle.

The Clerk rode in a chair carried by four sweating men. He went ahead of the cage up the zigzag path and Xantee felt him probing for ambushes Keech might set. She could have told him there were none. Only mice and lizards lived in the bushes on either side. She felt them draw deep into themselves as the Clerk went by. The cage had a roof of bars bent to meet in the centre, but the floor was timber and the shafts the men lifted with were made from gas-lamp poles torn down in the streets. The structure tipped on every corner and Xantee and Tarl held the bars to keep from sliding. The carriers stumbled and cursed. Duro and Danatok and the dogs climbed three turns below, keeping their minds veiled from the Clerk, keeping out of sight.

The Clerk had not spoken to her this morning. He had eaten soup the woman fed him in a spoon, and peed into a pot she held for him, and swallowed his potion, and fallen back into his drugged sleep. Xantee pitied him for the pain that stabbed his withered arm when he was awake. It almost made her understand his cruelty. But drugged or not he had the ability to spring into consciousness and be alert. Now, finding no ambush on the path, he slipped into a doze. His head lolled, the clawed hand clung like a bird to his cheek. Poor Clerk, she thought. Poor little man. It was not a thought she would allow herself when he was awake.

The path levelled out and joined a wide street. The bowmen scouted left and right. The heaviness in the air increased, which puzzled Xantee – shouldn't the breeze from the sea make things fresher? Then she understood – it was like a blow, knocking her thoughts askew and making her dizzy. *The gool was here. The gool lived on this hill.* She should have worked it out sooner. The mother gool would have her den, her hole, her hiding place, close to the clearing where Keech and the Clerk held their meetings, where the air about them, poisoned by their cruelty and greed, gave her the nourishment she needed.

Xantee gripped the bars and tried to hunt the creature down – was she in the tangle of trees on the other side of the street; was she in a hollow in the cliffs, or in the blackened ruins of one of the great houses? Wherever Xantee sent her mind she found emptiness. The gool must have defences. She must have ways of concealment, some barrier she raised. Perhaps with Duro's and Danatok's help . . .

'Girl,' cried the Clerk. She had forgotten him and some edge of her thoughts had brushed his mind, jerking him awake. She felt his attempt to burn her as he had burned Tarl, and she played her part, falling, screaming, and when he released her, lying curled on the floor, sobbing as though with pain and exhaustion.

I'm all right, she said urgently to Duro. He might come charging up the path.

The chair-carriers had turned the Clerk to face her. 'Who were you talking to, girl? Was it Keech?'

She rose to her knees, miming pain, and whispered just loud enough for him to hear: 'I was hunting the gool. She lives up here.'

'Ah, so you're back with your tale of monsters. You're a fool, girl. You're a child. You belong in the nursery.' He waved at the chairmen to turn him round, called to the bowmen: 'Watch her. Shoot if she tries any tricks.'

'Are you all right, Xantee?' Tarl said. She was pleased to hear him use her name. Usually it was 'girl', like the Clerk.

'I'm all right,' she said, and added in a whisper: 'He can't hurt me. I was pretending.'

182

'Then teach me to pretend.'

'There's no time.'

They crossed the wide street and the Clerk was alert again, searching for an ambush in the brushwood smothering the lawns. They went past a mound of charred timber and in a moment broke into an open space, behind a house leaning like a tree in a gale. Xantee knew, from Pearl's stories, that it was the Ottmar mansion, the only house to survive the wars. The lower part of the back wall was torn off, exposing staircases and water-ruined walls once lined with tapestries or painted with murals. Yet there was enough grandeur left to make the two petty kings choose it as their meeting place. They must feel puffed up here – although the reminder of luxuries they could not have must also increase their savagery.

A space had been chopped in the scrub. The ornate rim of a fountain showed through tangled vines. Frogs croaked inside, but fell silent as the Clerk's party approached. The bearers put down the chair and cage. They backed away round the side of the house, leaving the guards and prisoners and the Clerk, with his nurse crouched humbly at his side. He nudged her away with his toe.

'See, girl, Ottmar's house. See, dogman. Here is where your dogs killed Ottmar. And here is where you'll die, when I've shown you to Keech. He'll want you for himself, but you're mine.'

Tarl shook his head and made no reply. A stillness had fallen on him. He was remembering Hari, who had jumped from the cliff beyond the trees, holding Pearl's hand; who had died that day, and come back to life, and now lay dying again.

Xantee felt a whisper from Duro, circling clear of the Clerk: Are you all right?

He and Danatok had crept round the open space and hidden in trees by the cliff. When she had answered him – Yes, I'm all right – he sent her a picture of the marble hand that stood at the cliff-edge – shining white in Pearl's and Hari's tales, even when shattered by a cannon bolt, but now stained yellow and half-clothed in moss. She saw it was a place the gool might live, but hid the thought because she did not want Duro distracted. The Clerk and Keech must be dealt with first, then the gool.

The Clerk was alert. Xantee felt his distrust and his hatred of Keech. She felt schemes wriggling in his head, schemes for ambush, schemes for murder, but he could not make them settle and take shape. The Clerk was afraid of the burrows man and unsure that he could master him. It made him pucker his face and look at Tarl like a hungry child. Tarl he could master, he had no doubt of that.

'Clerk,' said the bowman leader, 'Keech is coming.'

'I can feel him. Who does he bring?'

Xantee felt Keech too and felt, like a punch, the prisoners he brought, and although sick with horror, was ready when he stepped from the scrub, behind his knife-guard. He led Sal and Mond on ropes tied around their necks. The cousins were bedraggled, beaten, bruised, but they still held hands.

Keech's eye found Tarl with a click-beetle jump and his hand fell to his knife, but the Clerk cried, 'No, Keech. He's mine. I branded him. See the name on his forehead. I put that there in Blood Burrow, in Ottmar's time, and it makes him mine. And see the girl. She runs with him. Runs with his dogs. I will punish Tarl but you can have the girl. She's my gift, but watch her, Keech; she can sneak inside your mind if you let her. She's a pretty thing, don't you think?'

Keech still had his eyes fixed on Tarl. 'I want no girl,' he said. 'Throw her off the cliff. But I'll give you these two as slaves' – jerking the ropes and making Sal and Mond stumble. 'They came to spy on me. They have a voice, the same as the girl, but feeble, like new-littered rats. I took them, Clerk, no trouble, and I've brought them here to show you – and now you show me Tarl in a cage. He's the one I want. Give him to me.'

They quarrelled like children, while the bowmen and knifemen eyed each other, ready to spring into action. Xantee was forgotten and she took the chance to speak with the cousins: Sal, Mond, listen. Duro and Danatok and the dogs are in the trees. Be ready when I call. Soon I'm going to talk with these men. You remember Barni's tale? The Clerk and Keech are the red star and the white. And the gool lives here, on the hill. Can you feel her lapping at them? Lapping the poison? I'll get them to help us and we'll send her back –

You can't, Sal and Mond said. They're not men any more. They're gools themselves. Kill them, Xantee. Kill them both. The gool will die.

No –

'Girl,' the Clerk cried, 'who are you talking to?'

'No one –'

Again he struck at her and again she writhed and howled. This time he kept on longer, to impress Keech. She knew that Duro, hidden in the trees, would hear her cries, and she risked sending a message: I'm all right. Stay hidden. Then she felt a burning behind her eyes, and realised that Keech had

185

joined the Clerk. They were competing to see who could hurt her most and some of the pain was edging through her defences. She concentrated, pushing it out, keeping it out, but the effort was so great – the attack coming, red, white, red, white, and sharp one moment, blunt the next – that she had no energy to writhe and scream . . .

'She's fainted,' said the Clerk. 'You thrash around like a beached whale, Keech. You hit with a club. The mind is a spear –'

'You've got nothing to teach me, Clerk. Let me have Tarl. Then you'll see how I make men howl.'

Again they argued.

Tarl was kneeling beside Xantee, brushing hair from her eyes. She felt for the first time that his mind was open to her, and she said silently: Tarl, I'm speaking to you. Say nothing. I'll stay like this for a moment. You can talk to me. Think what you want to say. Talk into my head.

She heard a whisper, as faint as an insect's wing brushing a curtain: Girl, Xantee, I can't do this.

Yes you can. Don't try, don't think, just talk inside your own head and mine at the same time.

I can't . . .

I can hear you. I'm going to wake up in a minute. I'm going to tell them about the gool. I can hear her feeding on them. If I can make them understand –

You can't. They don't care who dies, or if the world dies. They only care about themselves.

I'll try anyway.

And after that I'll kill them.

How, Tarl . . . ?

186

There was no more time. Keech and the Clerk had finished their snarling. Xantee let Tarl lift her to her feet.

'So, the dogman helps his sick bitch,' the Clerk said. 'Pull her out, bowmen, so I can give her to Keech. I've no use for the other two. Keep them, Keech. But tell me, why do you want this meeting? To show me your prisoners? Mine are better, the dogman and this girl, who's my gift to you. She looks like that Pearl who jumped with the dogman's son off the cliff. Blue eyes, see. Your two are vermin. They're slant-eyes. Use them to scrub your latrines.'

'It was you who wanted a meeting, Fat One. And I want no gift from you. Keep her to rub ointment on that claw you call a hand –'

'Stop,' Xantee shouted. Two men had hauled her from the cage, while others aimed their bows to keep Tarl inside and clanged the door. She stood up from the chopped scrub-stumps where they had thrown her. 'Stop,' she said more softly, but threw a hard command, like a stone, at each of them: Stop your talking. Listen to me.

The Clerk leaned forward in his chair, fixing her with his gaze, his good hand gripping Tarl's knife, which he had picked up to taunt Keech with; and Keech swivelled round on his bandy legs, like a wooden puppet, and clicked her into focus with his beetle eye.

'No woman talks to Keech like that,' he said, and slid his knife out of its ratskin sheath.

'Wait, Keech,' the Clerk said. 'She has a story to tell. You believe in monsters from the other world. You can listen to her around your fires at night, you and your men who tremble at the dark –'

'Clerk, I'll kill you soon.'

'Look at my men. Every bolt is aimed at you.'

'And my knife men have their blades ready to throw –'

'Stop,' Xantee repeated. 'You're doing the gool's work. Listen while I tell you Barni's tale. You Clerk, and you Keech, you're not monsters, you're men. This is your world. But you're letting this creature feed on you and make it hers. Her children are in the forests and the mountains. Every day they grow stronger. The forests fall before them, the mountains turn to dust, they drink the seas, they'll kill every living thing – and it all starts here, on this hill, with Keech and the Clerk, with your hatred and cruelty and malice and greed. That's the poison she feeds on. Can't you feel her sucking it out of you? You're the red star and the white. Barni's tale –'

'Enough,' said the Clerk.

'Shut the slut's mouth,' said Keech. 'You, One-eye, use your knife on her.'

When she thought about what happened next, Xantee could never place things in a sequence. Often she thought, yes, Duro, then Tarl, then the dogs, and Sal and Mond, but she could never decide who acted first. Her own part was to try and stop the killing, but she managed to save only one life. She remembered plainly, and always with horror, the man, Richard One-eye, advancing towards her with his knife balanced in his hand, his eye-socket hollow, with eyelids stitched together, and his good eye slick with anticipation. For a moment her mind failed to work, and she felt Keech and the Clerk, both aware of her strength, working to hold her – but she managed a command: Stop. Then everything happened at once.

One-eye stopped. Perhaps it was Xantee's command, perhaps Duro's knife, thrown from the trees, thudding into his side, up to the hilt, below his raised elbow. That was what she remembered first: the thud, the red squirt of blood painting One-eye's arm. But the dogs, Him and Her, materialised in the same moment, streaks of yellow and brown racing across the open space and leaping on the bowmen who kept Tarl covered. Too late. Both had released their cords. One bolt was deflected by a cage bar, but the other took Tarl – who had already jerked Xantee's knife from his sheath and thrown underhand between the bars; and quick as light the blade sped across the open space, over the head of the nurse at the Clerk's feet and struck the Clerk in the throat, high under his chin. The Clerk's eyes sprang wide with astonishment and his glasses slid down his nose. He toppled – but Xantee did not see him fall, or Tarl fall, or see the dogs biting the bars of the cage. Sal and Mond . . .

Keech had handed the ropes that held the cousins to the man Ratty, who dropped them when Duro's knife struck One-eye. All around, the guards began fighting, knifemen and bowmen attacking the enemies they knew; and Keech was using his knife, slashing at a man reloading his crossbow, driving him back. Sal and Mond snatched up a fallen rope, each one-handed, bent it in the air with a flick of their wrists, using the rope-skills of their people, jumped at Keech as though their limbs answered one set of commands, looped his head, thrust a foot each into his back, while jerking the rope, and broke his neck. As the Clerk toppled, Keech fell. (And somewhere close, yet far away, Xantee heard the gool's cry of agony and loss.)

Duro and Danatok were among the fighting men, stilling them; and Xantee seized those left, until they stood vacant-faced, with their weapons hanging at their sides.

It was only then that Xantee heard the howling. The dogs howled at the cage door. Inside Tarl lay dying. The nurse wailed, cradling the dead Clerk in her arms. And Sal, lying beside Mond on the ground, raised her voice in terrible grief. A crossbow bolt had taken Mond in the back, and she had whispered one word, 'Sal', before she died.

What happened next? Xantee's memory played things in a different order each time. She was kneeling beside Sal, comforting her, but Sal bit the hand that stroked her face, driving Xantee away. She was digging in the doublet of the dead leader of the guards, finding the cage key, flinging open the door. The dogs reached Tarl before she could move. They licked his face, they licked his wound, and snarled when she tried to pull the crossbow bolt from his chest. It would not have helped. Blood bubbled from Tarl's lips and he died. The dogs raised their muzzles and howled. Then she was struggling with the Clerk's nurse, who had found Tarl's knife beside the Clerk's body and was trying to plunge it into her own breast. Xantee could not get the knife from her so she stepped back and commanded: Sleep, and the woman slumped to the ground. Hers was the life Xantee saved.

Then, with Danatok helping, she entered Sal's mind and found it turbulent with grief that would destroy her. She and Danatok shut down the girl's consciousness and left her sleeping beside her cousin. They did not try to loosen her grip on Mond's hand.

The sun was high over Mansion Hill. A breeze came from the sea. But still the air was thick with the presence of the gool. And now something was added: the creature's smell.

It must mean she's dying, Duro said.

There was no time to hunt for her. Wounded men were groaning on the ground. Xantee and Danatok disarmed the guards they had immobilised, then woke them and set them to work. There was nothing for dressing wounds and no medicine for pain, but they tore rough bandages from the clothing of dead men, and by mid-afternoon had sent the surviving guards and the wounded down the hill. Ratty, with a crossbow bolt in his stomach, rode in the Clerk's chair. The nurse, half-woken from her sleep, trailed after them.

Xantee looked around. Tarl's body lay in the cage. The dogs would not let anyone near. The Clerk was curled on his side, like a brightly dressed doll laid down to sleep. Keech was stretched out, his head thrown back, his good eye glaring at the sun. Six other dead men lay in the clearing.

Now, Duro said, we find this gool.

No, Xantee said, we'll talk with the twins and find out how Hari is. She turned her back on the dead and went to the other side of the fountain. Duro and Danatok followed. She felt Duro's mind jumping about, fizzing with the excitement of the fight.

Duro, she said, if you want to help you'll have to calm down.

I want this gool.

After we've talked to the twins.

She slipped her mind into Danatok's and in a moment felt Duro join them. All three together, they called out to Hubert and Blossom. The twins were waiting.

191

Xantee, what's happening?

We found the red star and the white. They're both dead. Was it in time? Is Hari alive?

Yes. He's breathing. He's getting more air. The thing around his neck gave a jerk and it rolled over. It cried out. It's looser now and Hari can breathe. But Xantee, it won't let go. We've tried to cut it and burn it and we've all worked together, telling it to release him, but it's hanging on. We think it's putting some sort of poison into Hari because he's starting to sweat and tremble. We don't know what it means, except Pearl and Tealeaf say the gool's not dead. You've got to find her, Xantee. You've got to kill her. And do it quickly or Hari will die.

She's here on the hill, Xantee said. Stay with Hari. We'll find her.

The three unravelled their voices. They opened their eyes and looked at each other.

Where? Duro said.

Here, Danatok replied. He looked around helplessly. But she's hiding and there's a lot of ground to search.

Xantee shook her head.

We don't need to, she said. All we've got to do is follow her smell.

FOURTEEN

It led them into Ottmar's mansion. They went through long
bare rooms with their ceilings collapsed and rotting tapestries hunched at the foot of walls. They crept past fallen
chandeliers, heaped on the floor like forgotten treasure, and
broken tables, and upholstered chairs with their seats ripped
open and their stuffing piled like foam. Stairways led to open
spaces where spider nests clung to the walls. But the gool was
down. Her smell was buried under the floor – and less heavy
as they went towards the front of the house.

They turned back through the wide rooms to the rear
entrance hall. The smell was thickest there.

It's down. She's there, Xantee said, pointing at a narrow
stairway turning into the dark. Again she remembered her
parents' story: the stairs led to the servants' quarters, where
Ottmar had stored his poison salt.

Dark, Duro said. He hated the dark and felt for his knife,
but it was still embedded in the man called One-eye.

They found dry wood and made three torches. Danatok led the way down the stairs. The torches threw multiple soft shadows and the darkness beyond seemed spongy and wet. They advanced cautiously, not knowing if the gool would be in the open or hidden, not knowing her shape or size, and if she would attack or try to escape. But she was here. They felt her now – her presence, her malevolence and fear.

She's different, Xantee whispered. She's different from the ones we saw.

She's afraid, Danatok said.

And she's bloody dangerous, Duro said.

The stairs ended. They went through a door hanging crooked on its hinges. Beyond their pocket of light the torches showed a hill of broken tables and chairs. If the gool was as big as her children, as big as the one in the mountain pass, she would fill this room. But she was not here. Xantee could feel her through the wall – concentrated, wrapped in a ball.

She's small, she whispered. She's a small thing.

And dangerous, Duro repeated.

She's in the next room, Danatok said.

Xantee remembered her parents' story again. There were two corridors outside the eating room: a narrow one leading to a side door and, at right angles, a wider one to a wider door. The first opened into a washroom lined with latrines, the second into a dormitory that, in Pearl and Hari's day, had been emptied of beds and set up as a factory for Ottmar's poison bullets.

They went past the jumble of beds and tables, out of the eating hall, and chose the corridor leading straight ahead. It seemed safer simply because it was wide. Their feet whispered on the gritty floor. Their torches pushed the darkness back like skeins of wool and seemed to pile it at the corridor's end. The door into the dormitory was jammed half open. Someone had drawn a skull on it with charcoal. Someone else had made the skull cry, with fat blood-red tears dropping down. But this whole downstairs space where the servants had lived gave the impression of being unscavenged and unexplored. Not even burrows men came here.

Duro edged into the dormitory, holding a club-shaped bed leg he had found by the door. Xantee and Danatok followed. A wooden table on trestles ran half the length of the room. There were no chairs and the table was bare except for two small balls, crouching like mice. Duro laid down his club and picked one up.

Heavy, he said.

Ottmar's lead bullets, Xantee said. They were supposed to have poison salt in them. Put it down, Duro.

She was finding it hard to breathe. The smell of the gool was even thicker in this room. It was slippery, spreading on her skin like oil.

Duro put the bullet down. He gave a muffled cry. Two still figures lay on the other side of the table. Two dead men.

Again it was Xantee who understood. Not men. These long grey figures with rigid limbs were the lead suits Ottmar's salt technicians had worn to protect themselves. They must have shed them here before they ran to escape his anger.

She calmed Duro. His fears were increasing every moment they spent in this underground place. He wanted to fight an enemy he could see and understand.

Meanwhile, Danatok had explored the room.

Here, he called.

He stopped before an iron safe bolted to the wall and leaned at it, feeling with his mind but keeping clear. Xantee and Duro approached, and felt at once why he did not go closer. He would have to swim through the smell of the gool like water, and chop and tear his way through her barrier of hatred – hatred of everything in this world not hers. It churned their stomachs and sickened their minds and they stood unable to move.

She's in there, Xantee whispered.

Can she hurt us? Duro said. He was swaying as though he might fall.

She hurts us just by being herself, Danatok said.

The safe door was an inch or two ajar. Something oozed out: darkness that ran like a liquid and made a hissing like steam. It made their torches spit and tremble, and burn with a colour none of them had ever seen. It slid along their faces as though tasting their lips and eyes.

Duro, off to one side, reeled back, turned his back, gave a sob of pain. He whacked the thickened air with his club.

Duro, Danatok said, find a long piece of wood. Bring it back here.

Duro stumbled away behind his torch.

She's strong, Xantee said. But she's wounded. Killing Keech and the Clerk was like tearing something out of her.

But she won't die, Danatok said.

She's trying to find other things to feed on, Xantee said.

They heard Duro rummaging in the pile of beds by the latrines. He came back dragging a length of timber with a

196

bolt protruding from one end. He had dropped his club but kept his torch.

Now, Danatok said, stand to one side. Use it to push the door open.

He and Xantee stood back. Duro put down his torch and fitted the bolt against the edge of the safe door. It slid off when he started to push. He reversed the timber and used the thicker end. The door was stiff, its hinges groaned. And something else groaned, low in the safe. The sound made Xantee's skin prickle and her mouth go dry. It did not come from grief or anger or any emotion she could recognise. It was a sound no one was meant to hear, from a darkness no one was meant to see.

The hinge ran free, the door clanged open and a concentrated beam of hatred shot out and knocked Xantee and Danatok off their feet. It rolled them like logs on the floor. Somehow Danatok kept his torch alive. Duro, off to the side, snatched up his and moved to thrust it into the safe, but Xantee, jammed against the trestle legs, cried, No, stay back. She felt as if the gool's hatred was tearing off her skin, but she managed to roll to one side of the invisible beam.

Danatok.

Yes, he answered weakly, and crawled after her.

Duro was on the other side. Crossing to them would be like stepping into the heat-blast from a furnace. Yet there was nothing to see. The gool stayed hidden at the back of the safe that was her home.

Xantee lit her dead torch at Danatok's.

We've got to see her, she said. And then we've got to send her back.

If we join our minds, all three . . .

And make a shield. We should be able to keep her away from us. Duro, are you ready?

Ready, he gasped.

They folded their minds together and made their shield, visualising it – a sheet of light, as strong as iron, standing between them and the gool. Then, Xantee and Danatok from the right, Duro from the left, they stepped in front of the safe.

The gool's hatred beat against the shield and buckled it, made dents the size of fists in its surface, but their minds kept it steady and inched it towards the open door. The torch-light mingling with the silver shine of the shield penetrated the safe. They saw the gool.

She was nothing like her children. Xantee thought at first she was a pile of rags, but that lasted only a second. Her hatred had the weight of an avalanche. It beat on their shield, sharp and blunt, like an axe one moment and a club the next, but they held steady, keeping their minds plaited like three ropes, keeping their gaze firm and their torches high, and studied her.

Not rags, Xantee thought. That had been an effect of the shadows. She was smooth and small and fat and grey, like a gourd taken from a vine – like an unripe gourd picked and stored for some reason in this safe. But that likeness would not do, for her smoothness was sticky and her greyness was transparent and something moved inside her, rolling and twisting like eels in a sack, making her lumpy, then moving deeper and sucking hollows in her skin. Heart perhaps, lungs perhaps, beating and breathing, and stomach and intestines, black and grey – but that too could not be right, for she had no mouth, no way to eat, and no nose to breathe through. Perhaps she breathed through her skin for it seemed to open and close in a thousand black pores, almost too fast to be seen.

She had no arms or legs, no limbs at all, breaking the swollen end of her gourd shape, and nothing at the thinner end, although some hidden part made a ticking sound and something protruded, no thicker than a wire, linking her, Xantee guessed, to the world she came from.

She had eyes. They floated inside her, white cloudy discs, deep one moment, shallow the next, and because there were two and because they watched, they became the focus of Xantee's and Duro's and Danatok's attention.

They took a step closer, breathing lightly to stop her smell from overpowering them.

Gool, they said, speaking with Xantee's voice. Gool, it's time for you to go.

The creature had no language. All she had was hatred – hatred and enormous strength. It rolled from her in waves, rolled over them, but they braced themselves and held their ground, and Xantee said, Gool, your food is gone. The Clerk is dead. Keech is dead. The red star and the white that kept you nourished are gone. There's nothing left to eat any more. No hatred. No cruelty. It died with them, and you'll die if you stay here. Go back where you live. You and your children can't have our world.

Still hatred rolled off the gool.

Does she understand? Duro said.

I heard her laugh when you told her there was no hatred left, Danatok said.

What can we do?

Force her back. Pick her up and throw her through whatever hole she came from, Duro said.

It won't work, Xantee said. We've got to make her afraid of staying.

We've got to kill her, that's what, Duro said. Give me your knife, Danatok.

Before Danatok had time to answer, Duro snatched it from the Dweller's sheath, stepped out from the shield and threw in a single motion at the gool in her den. The knife struck between her floating eyes and sank in – and kept on sinking, blade and handle, until it disappeared. The gool's eyes rolled over, then steadied and fixed on Duro. He stepped back behind the shield as a blast of hatred leapt at him. It clanged like a rain of spears but Xantee and Danatok held their cover firm.

She swallowed it, Duro whispered. She swallowed the knife.

We can't kill her that way, Danatok said.

She's stronger, Xantee said. Every time we try to kill her she'll get stronger. It's why she laughed. The Clerk and Keech fed her but she can survive even though they're dead. All the bits of cruelty in our world are food for her. She can't be killed.

We've got to try. Let's take her down to the sea and drown her. Or throw her off the cliff. Or make a fire . . .

She's laughing, Danatok said.

And that thing round Hari's neck is still alive. It'll never die, Xantee whispered.

So what do we do?

I don't know. But she's afraid of us. So there must be a way.

200

She looked at the gool. It looked back at her, turning the discs that served as eyes.

Go home, she whispered. Please. It's not your world. She made a tipping gesture with her hand, as though sliding the gool into its place, and acknowledging that perhaps the gool heard a voice there that spoke its name, and everything it felt might be natural. Then she remembered *her* voice, the great voice, which said 'Xantee'; which spoke – she was sure now – from a place of light opposing the gool's darkness. She tried to hear it. There was only silence. Xantee, she said to herself, trying to command it. The silence went on – and deep in the gool she heard the gulping sound of its laughter.

Gool, she pleaded: but it was invulnerable. There was enough hatred in the world to feed it forever, and help it breed even more children. Hatred in the city, in the burrows: and hatred in Duro and, she supposed, herself. She was no different from anyone else. And so the gool could sip at her, and sip at her . . .

Xantee stared at the creature. It stared back at her.

You don't have any other feelings, she whispered. This bulging sticky fat thing, with its blank eyes and surging hatred and huge greed, had no other feelings. I hate you, she thought, but as well as that . . . She was overwhelmed with pity for the things it could never know.

I don't think you're really alive, she whispered.

She put out her hand, pushing it through the shield that kept them safe.

Go back, she said. Go back where it doesn't matter.

Silence. It was as if the world had stopped turning. Then there was a creaking, a groaning, and a crack like the breaking of a giant tree. The sound turned over, leaving a new silence that shivered with intensity. And growing out of it came a whimper, a baby's whimper, as if the gool had drawn some knowledge into herself and disbelieved it. Xantee, Duro, Danatok could not breathe. A voice, not human, in a language not human, cried a single word they understood. *No*, it cried. Then a rumbling and splashing filled the room, as though a cliff was sliding into the sea. Deep in her head Xantee heard something scream, and scream again, and again. The sound fell gradually away, as though tumbling down long stairs into the dark. Soon it became a piteous mewing. Her own, her great voice, spoke to her, regretful and firm. She knew then that pity had been a weapon. Where Duro's knife had failed, and flame and poison and spears would fail, pity had pierced the gool and made it shriek. Now the creature's eyes rolled like wheels, she trembled and convulsed. She writhed in her den, making its iron walls bulge. Her eyes dulled and sank, fluttering like discs of tin deep in a pool, and her body sagged and seemed to melt.

'What's happening?' Duro cried.

She's dying, Danatok said.

'Why? How?'

Danatok made no reply. He withdrew from the shield and Duro lurched after him. Xantee stepped out too and let the shield fall. She could not speak, could not explain, but sank to her knees and hugged her arms across her chest, trying to keep her own warmth in as the gool died. She had killed this creature, although it trembled and loosened still. Killed it without meaning to, by striking pity into it like a knife. She did not want to understand; but watched the gool, feeling its agony and trying to hasten its end.

The gool died, with a final shudder and a childlike sob. At once its skin began to curl and flake. A foul smell drove Duro and Danatok backwards, and Danatok pulled Xantee to her feet as he went. He pushed her, stumbling, to the door. They ran from the room. The smell followed, enfolding them and wetting their faces. They reached the steps, stumbled up, and burst from the ruined mansion into the air – where a breeze from the sea turned the stench away and carried it over the city. They ran past the fountain to the cage where Tarl lay and the dogs watched, and the open space with the dead men sleeping in a row, and Sal lying beside her cousin on the grass.

What happened? Duro said again.

I think she died because I pitied her, Xantee said.

Duro shook his head. He did not understand.

Does it mean the other gools are dead?

I don't know. Let's talk to the twins.

They were still trembling with horror, and trying to wipe the smell of the gool off themselves, so reaching the farm was harder. But they steadied their minds and found Blossom and Hubert waiting.

Hari? Is Hari all right? Xantee said.

Yes. The thing's gone from his neck. It gave a squeak like a mouse and rolled over, and then it melted – but the stink! We've carried Hari out of there. Pearl and Tealeaf are washing him in the tub. What happened, Xantee?

The gool's dead. The mother's dead. And I think all the others, everywhere, must be dying.

She did not know how the mother had kept them alive;

but threads, perhaps no more than threads of thought, perhaps of a strange kind of love, went out from her to her offspring and her death flowed along them to wherever the children were. Her pain was theirs and her dying theirs.

Karl and some of the others are taking the schooner, the twins said. They'll see if the gool Sal and Mond found is dead. Xantee, there's so much going on here –

Yes, here too. Tell Hari we love him. Tell Pearl.

And tell my ma, Duro said.

They gathered dry timber from the house and built a pyre. Xantee controlled the dogs while Duro and Danatok carried Tarl from the cage and laid him on it. Duro placed Tarl's knife on his chest. They broke Mond's hand from Sal's, tearing the skin, and laid her beside Tarl. When the fire was blazing, Xantee woke Sal and held her lightly, but released her when she saw Sal understood. The dogs howled. Sal sang a dirge in a tongue only she understood. The pyre collapsed and when the bodies were reduced to charred bones in the embers, the dogs turned and ran soundlessly. They vanished round the fountain.

Where are they going? Duro said.

Back to the forest.

Sal sat by the embers and bowed her head.

They left her there and dragged the Clerk and Keech into the mansion and laid them side by side in the room with the fallen chandeliers. Then they dragged the dead men in and put them in a row, burrows men with city men. Duro and Danatok circled the outside walls, setting fires, and soon the mansion was ablaze. They did not stay to see it fall, but raised Sal to her feet and set off for Port.

The gool smell, turning in the smoke, faded away.

FIFTEEN

They reached Port at midday the next day. Behind them, the burrows were quiet. A haze of smoke drifted over the city from Mansion Hill but the air was fresh beside the water. They swam in the sea, washing the last smell of the gool out of their clothes, but Xantee could not wash the creature out of her mind.

She's left some of herself in me, she thought.

Danatok rowed them to his stilt house and they rested for three days. On the second they concentrated their minds and spoke with the twins. Hari was growing stronger, Blossom and Hubert said. He was able to whisper a few words.

Don't tell him Tarl's dead, Xantee said.

Karl had not reached the place where Sal and Mond had found their gool, but Xantee was not interested. She knew all the gools were dead. Whatever flowed to them from their mother was cut off. Like her they would fall shapeless and rot away.

On the third day they prepared to leave. Danatok was staying. Although he did not say so, he needed to be alone. He scouted the shoreline and found a canoe he could patch. It was enough. Xantee and Duro could take his boat.

They fitted it with a mast and sail, loaded it with provisions and water, enough for two days, and set off on the fourth morning, with Danatok beside them until they were out of the harbour. They called goodbye and he turned the canoe away.

The boat was heavy and the sail small, but Duro and Xantee were good sailors. They took turns at the tiller. Sal sat in the bow, taking no part. She had not spoken a word since singing her dirge for Mond. The bleeding on her palm had stopped but the flesh was raw. She hid her hand in her armpit whenever Xantee tried to bandage it.

They sailed for fourteen days, sleeping on beaches, foraging for food and taking water from streams.

Saltport slid past. Its buildings were empty and the dead hill behind it wore a scar. Xantee scarcely looked. The place was in Pearl's and Hari's life, not in hers.

Dwellers had gathered on the beach at Stone Creek. They welcomed and fed the travellers, and gave them news: Karl had found the gool. It had fallen to a puddle of sludge, turning to dust at the edges. And Dwellers in touch with the people with no name made the same report: the gools were dead.

Good, Duro said.

Xantee nodded. It was good. And Hari grew stronger, the Dwellers reported. That was good too. But she could not be happy. She was pining for her brother, Lo. There was no news of him.

Dwellers guided them eastwards through the forests. The people with no name kept them safe in the jungle. When Xantee asked about Lo they retreated. She stopped using his name and asked about the human boy with the shattered leg. The people said they had no knowledge of him.

Tealeaf and Karl met them at the Inland Sea. They were full of praise and bursting with talk of Hari and Pearl and Tilly and the village. Tealeaf took Sal under her care but could not penetrate her trance or make her speak.

They sailed home. Hari and Pearl and the twins were waiting on the beach. Tilly was there. Xantee felt something like happiness at last. There was embracing, and talk, and rejoicing late into the night, and food and drink, and village folk coming until midnight to welcome the travellers and praise them – and yes, Xantee was happy. Her father was recovered. There was a white scar round his neck and his steps were slower and his hair had turned grey, and there was a quietness in his mind, a place of sorrow for his father. Pearl was blooming, she was beautiful, but the same sorrow lived in her. They had lost their son.

Xantee thought of all she had done – she and Duro. She tried not to be too pleased with herself, but could not stop it – she was pleased, she overflowed with amazement now and then. But two things always halted her: Lo gone. And her love for Duro, which on the journey home had seemed to fade away, then grow and fade again, and never settle. The pain it caused him had been her pain too.

So it went on. The summer went on. The farm and village flourished. Hari grew stronger, Pearl sang and played her flute, and Tealeaf came and went like a protective spirit. But

Sal stayed silent; and Xantee and Duro could be no more than friends.

Then, one sunny morning, a boy walked out of the forest and through the village, a boy with a limp. His hair was shaggy, he wore no clothes, he carried nothing. There was a smile on his lips.

'Lo?' said the villagers.

He made no answer but walked to the farm.

Pearl saw him from the porch. Her cry brought Xantee running from the gardens at the back.

Lo, she cried.

Pearl ran down the steps and caught the boy in her arms. Xantee hugged him, tears running down her cheeks. Hari came and took his son in his arms. The boy hugged them back, but it was as if he had learned how to do it. He stood away.

Lo, they said.

He smiled. I have no name.

But you've come back. You've come home to stay with us? Pearl cried.

My home is the jungle, the boy said. I've come because of your sorrow. I've come because you mustn't be unhappy.

Hari was the first to understand.

You live with the people? he said.

Yes, said the boy.

And you're one of them?

I'm one of them.

No, Pearl cried.

Yes, he said.

Are you happy with them? Xantee said.

I'm happy with them.

And you're going back?

The boy nodded. He stepped further away, as though to let them see it was true – he was happy and would go back. Pearl ran at him with her arms out. He stopped her by raising his hand – but touched her palm with his for a moment. Then he smiled again.

I'll take her with me. The one who is broken in half.

He found Sal standing at the edge of the sea. Xantee did not hear what he said – perhaps it was nothing. He put out his hand. Sal raised her eyes and looked at him. She took her scarred hand out of her armpit, studied it a moment, laid it on her cheek as though to cool it, then quietly placed it in his.

They walked up past the farmhouse and through the fields and into the forest, not looking back.

Oh, Pearl wept. Hari held her in his arms.

After that Xantee found she could love Duro. Their wedding was held in the farmhouse. In the morning they chose a boat from the shore and sailed away on their nuptial voyage.

The seasons went on. There were children. There was much happiness.

No new gool has found its way into their world.

THE FIRST INSTALMENT OF MAURICE GEE'S
BREATHTAKING *SALT* SERIES

Hari lives in Blood Burrow, deep in the ruined city of Belong, where he survives by courage and savagery. He is scarred from fighting, but he has a secret gift: he can speak with animals.

Pearl is from Company, the ruling families, which has conquered and enslaved Hari's people. Pampered and beautiful, she is destined for a marriage that will unite her family with that of the powerful and ambitious Ottmar. But Pearl has learned forbidden things from Tealeaf, her maid, and so the two must run.

Hari and Pearl forge an unusual alliance and become reluctant travelling companions. As the two come to grips with their strengthening powers, their quest evolves into a desperate pilgrimage to save the world from a terror beyond their greatest imaginings.

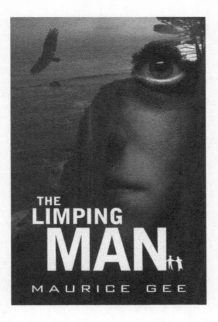

THE THIRD INSTALMENT OF MAURICE GEE'S
BREATHTAKING *SALT* SERIES

What is the source of the Limping Man's monstrous power?
Nobody can withstand it, a soft crawling that seeps into your
skin and wriggles into your mind, making you powerless with
love for him even as his cruelties multiply.

When Hana's mam chooses to swallow frogweed poison
rather than die in the great witch-burning in People's Square,
Hana flees the burrows before she too is taken. Deep in the
forest she meets Ben, son of Lo, and the two journey back to
the burrows to find a way to destroy the Limping Man before
his evil consumes the world.

But first they must discover the secret of his strength.

PRAISE FOR *GOOL*

'Even scarier than its predecessor. Gee's imagination is as fierce as ever.'

Herald on Sunday

'In *Gool*, the looming apocalypse has taken an almost mythical form . . . Gee is a master storyteller'

NZ Herald

'. . . a superb fantasy which turns the raw materials of legend into a dramatic and thought-provoking adventure'

Trevor Agnew, Magpies

'Xantee and Lo, son and daughter of Hari and Pearl (from the first title in this trilogy, *Salt*), set out on a perilous mission through jungles and mountains to find and kill the 'Gool' that is threatening Hari's life. It takes them to the scenes of their parents' past lives where they must confront the Company and finish what Hari and his father started years ago. This well-written, engrossing story uncontrivedly incorporates elements of *Salt*, last year's category winner. Allusive and metaphorical, *Gool* also offers readers characters who are humanly frail yet resilient in the face of an almost impenetrable darkness.'

Judges' Report, New Zealand Post Book Awards for Children and Young Adults, 2009